HIJACKED

A Beechwood Adventure

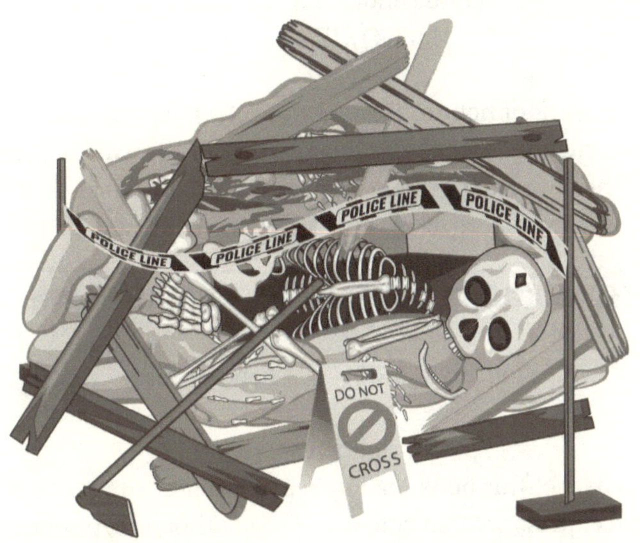

G Michael Smith

INDIEOWL
PRESS

4700 Millenia Blvd
Ste 175 #90776
Orlando, FL 32839

info@indieowlpress.com
IndieOwlPress.com

HIJACKED: A BEECHWOOD ADVENTURE

Illustrated by G Michael Smith

Edited by Vanessa Anderson at NightOwlFreelance.com

Cover art/design © G Michael Smith
Interior layout/design by Vanessa Anderson

ISBN-13: 978-1-949193-85-5

For Cheryl who shows me

all those things more valuable than gold.

"Ever tried. Ever failed. No matter.

Try Again. Fail again. Fail better."

– Samuel Beckett

Contents

CONTENTS

CONTENTS

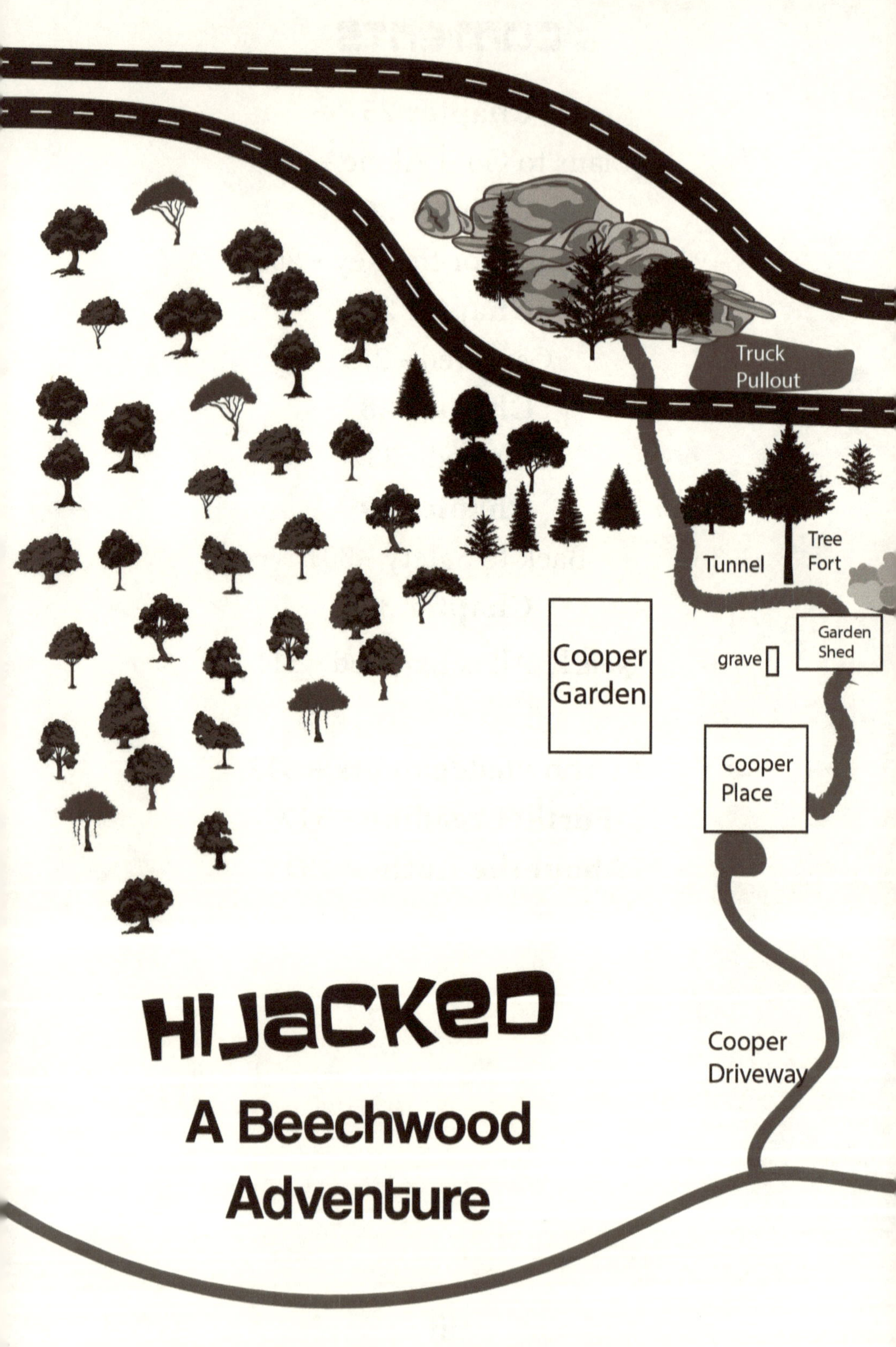

HIJACKED

A Beechwood Adventure

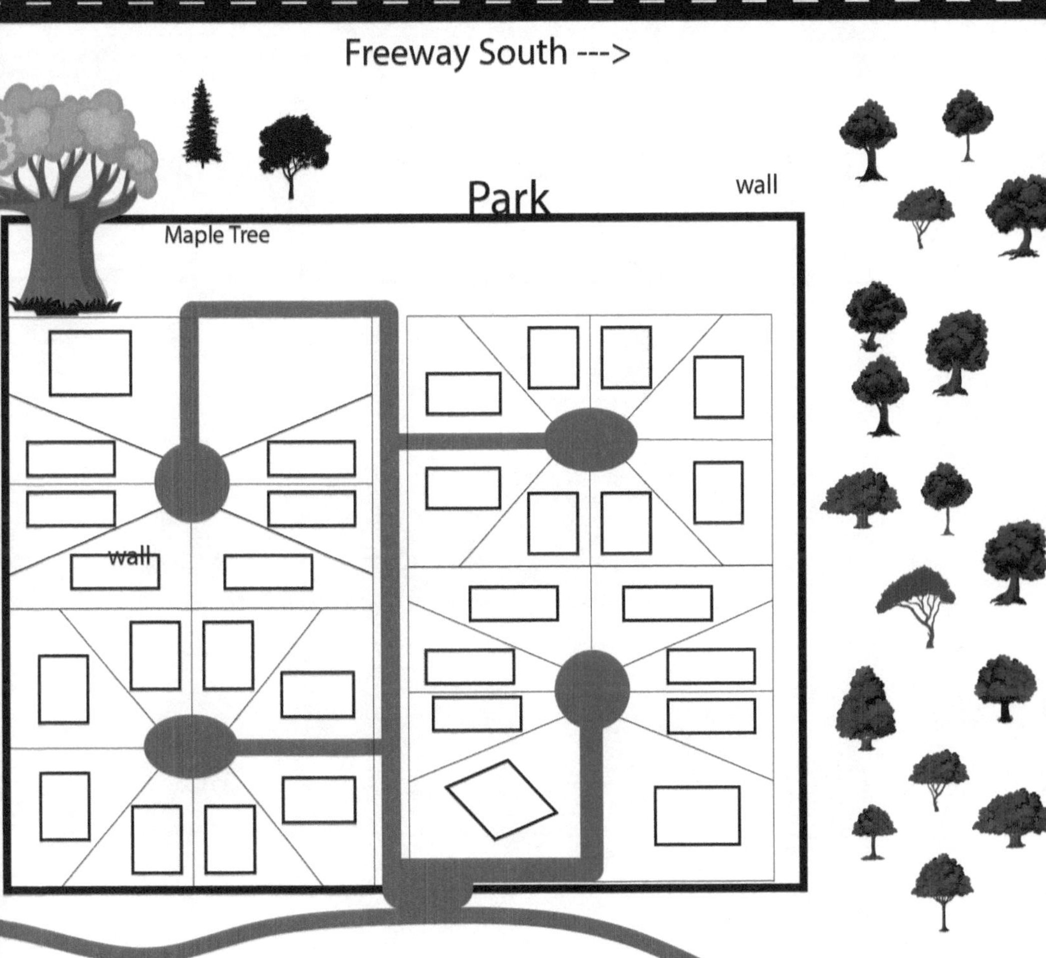

The Cornborough Estates
Freeway South --->
Maple Tree
Park
wall
wall
Beechwood Glen

a

very

sour

morning

CHAPTER 1

"William. William. William—wake up," called William's father from the kitchen.

William groaned and rolled over, mashing the pillow into his face. He tried to shut out the sound and recapture the dream. His mind drifted back to the field on the edge of the wood. The grass was cold. He could feel it wet against his cheek as he crawled forward on his elbows, army style. He stopped every few minutes and listened and rested. Whenever he stopped, his men also stopped. He could hear them breathing behind him. They were a team; one unit working together. He was proud to lead them. He had to get to the cave where they would be safe. Once they were in the cave they could barricade the opening and keep the zombies out. He could hear the zombies moan as they wandered aimlessly about. If the zombies found them, they would have to fight. All they had for weapons were small alder branches with spikes at one end. He knew how to handle himself, but he wasn't so sure about the rest of the guys. Zombies were hard to stop; after all, they were already dead.

"Ahhhrrrggg...Grrraaaa," moaned an old woman who appeared right in front of them. Her mouth sagged open so that her chin almost touched her neck. "Williammmmmm. Willll yaaaammmm geeeeeeetttttttttttuuuuuuuuuuupp," the sound gurgled out of her throat as the spit dripped from her sagging bottom lip.

Suddenly, the old woman zombie turned and jumped on William's back and pushed him into the soft ground. William screamed, pushed her away, and opened his eyes. He sat up quickly and looked at his father.

"William! Get out of bed—now!" his father ordered. "I have to go over to the Cooper place this morning, and you have to come with me."

"Do I have to?" whined William.

"You have to. Now get up and eat," said his father. "I have to get the tools in the truck."

"What's for breakfast?" William moaned from underneath the sheet he had pulled over his head.

His dad turned in the doorway. "Whatever you can fix and eat in 10-minutes 'cause that's how much time you have."

"I want blueberry pancakes," William shouted as he quickly sat up in bed.

His dad moved to the foot of the bed. He was wearing a t-shirt with "Chevys Rule" on the front. It used to be white. Now it was grey with green and brown stains across the front where he wiped his hands. It had not been washed for at least a week. That's how long his mother had been gone. His jeans were black. They had not started out that color. "I'm not your mother. You can talk her into making pancakes when she gets home. Make toast or cereal. I don't have time, especially when you sleep in," said his father with his hands on his hips.

"Mom and Jillian won't be home for like forever. By then I won't even remember what pancakes are. Please, Dad?" pleaded William.

"They'll be back in six weeks. You will survive until then," his father said sharply. "You now have eight minutes, or you go without breakfast."

"All right!" William snapped. He got out of bed and went into the bathroom. William's mom had gone to Europe with his older sister. William's Aunt Beth was a photographer and was working in Eastern Europe for the summer photographing castles. She had invited Valerie and Jillian to spend the summer with her. The only good thing about their trip was the absence of Jillian. She could stay in Europe forever for all William cared. Jillian was not William's favorite person. Valerie was William's mom's name. She made the best pancakes, especially during blueberry season. William loved blueberry pancakes more than just about anything else. The thought made his mouth water. "I'll never have blueberry pancakes for the whole summer," he thought, splashing water onto his face. He rubbed dry with the towel, ran his fingers through his hair and got dressed for work. He would have to "rake, wheel, and dump" – "rake, wheel, and dump." That was his job whenever his dad worked at the old Cooper place. His dad was renovating inside, landscaping the whole backyard, cleaning and fixing the gutters and painting just about everything. Mrs. Cooper was moving in at the end of the summer and his Dad had gotten the contract to fix the place up. William got a contract to be his Dad's labor force, and he had not even signed anything. It just wasn't fair. Every other kid in Beechwood had their summer free to do whatever they wanted but not Billy B. Oh no, not him. He was a prisoner. A prisoner in a labor camp who would never get blueberry pancakes ever again.

William Earle Braithwaite was technically his full name. He was named after his grandfather on his mother's side. William Earle is what his mother (and yucky sister) called him whenever they wanted to make him feel stupid. William Earle was the worst name anyone could ever have, and it was his. He hated it. "William" was bad enough, but the "Earle" part was just too much to take. He wanted to be called Billy or Billy B or Bad Billy or Bodacious Billy or Big Bad Bill or just about anything with Bill or Billy in it. All his friends called him Billy but no one in his family would. "I christened you *William Earle* and that's what I will call you. Believe me when I tell you that you will thank me when you are older," his mother would always say. So, no one inside his home would ever call him anything but William.

"William! Three minutes!" his father yelled.

Billy quickly pulled on his sneakers and ran into the kitchen. Cheerios was his only choice. He dumped some into a bowl, opened the fridge, grabbed the milk and poured the last of it over the cereal. He grabbed a spoon and shoveled it into his mouth. Three minutes, he thought, *was more than enough time to eat his cereal.*

Suddenly, Billy gagged. He ran to the sink and with one fluid motion he dumped the cereal, spit his mouthful into the sink, turned on the tap, sucked in and spit water back into the sink in an effort to clean the foul taste from his mouth.

"DAD!" he yelled after spitting for the fifth time. "The milk is sour! I thought you were getting fresh milk."

"Not my job," his father called from the garage. "You know where the house money is. You drink milk. Buy some."

"What am I going to eat?" yelled Billy.

"Not my problem," his father called back. "You got two-minutes. And don't think I am going to leave you behind. When I leave you are coming with me, breakfast or no breakfast."

Billy opened the fridge and grabbed an apple. He quickly searched the pantry and stuffed a granola bar in his pocket. He dashed toward the door to the garage. He heard his father's truck start. He screeched to a stop, bit down on the apple and held it in his mouth, ran back, grabbed a banana, ran out and jumped into the truck just as his father was slowly pulling away.

The "Cooper Place" was just outside Beechwood Glen or "The Glen" as everyone called the housing subdivision on the west side of the freeway. Billy lived in Beechwood Glen all his life. He knew every nook and cranny of the place.

The subdivision backed right onto the freeway. It was separated by a concrete fence covered with vines. The fence was supposed to keep anyone from wandering out onto the freeway, especially little kids on tricycles who didn't know any better. It was also supposed to keep the traffic noise down. Billy had never noticed the traffic noise. It also separated the subdivision from the Cooper Place. In fact, the subdivision, the freeway and the subdivision on the east side of the freeway all used to be part of the Cooper Place. It was chopped up when they put the freeway through. Before that it had apple, cherry, and plum orchards and a rooming house for miners and lumberjacks. All that had changed. It was now just the Cooper Place that backed onto the freeway on the west side, the Beechwood Glen beside the Cooper Place, the freeway, and Cornbourgh Estates on the east side of the freeway.

Billy's father pulled into the long winding driveway leading down to the old Cooper house and garden. It was a 10-minute drive from their house but a 5-minute walk if you knew the shortcut. The shortcut was a secret. Only Billy and the rest of the Beechwood Braves knew the shortcut. Billy thought about the gang and their upcoming meeting. It was set for 3:30. His father usually took him out for lunch but this afternoon he had an appointment with a client and was leaving Billy to work on his own until 2:00 in the afternoon. After that, he was free to meet with

"The Braves" – "The Beechwood Braves." That is what they were called. They were the best and he was their leader. Vince Patterson used to be the leader, but his family had moved away. After that, they had elected him. The thought made him smile.

The truck door on his father's side slammed shut. "Come on. Time's a-wastin'," his father said. That was what he always said before he started something.

Billy got his gloves, pushed the wheelbarrow full of tools over to the garden and started to hoe and pull weeds. It would take forever to pull out all the weeds from this gigantic ancient garden. Weed patch was a better term because that is all there were. WEEDS. He had asked his father one day why he didn't just rent a tiller and do it in an afternoon. He replied that tillers cost money and why would he spend money when he could get it done for free. He laughed and tousled Billy's hair. Billy had not laughed. Billy chopped at a giant thistle. He cut it off 3 cm from the ground. He whispered, "Timmmberrrr," to himself as the thistle fell.

"You gotta get the root. Dig down and get the root first. If you just chop it off it will be back next week, and you will have to do it again. If you dig down now it will be easier in the long run," his father said.

"It will take me forever. This ground has not been dug in like a thousand years. Look!" said Billy as he chopped at the base of the fallen thistle. "There's more than just thistle roots down there."

"There sure is. See those trees—the maple and the cedars. They both love water and send out root tendrils everywhere. This old garden is full of them," he lectured as he took the hoe from Billy. "You have to chop like this and take a little patch of earth at a time. Chop and pull out the roots. And go nice and deep. Like this," he demonstrated by chopping for a few seconds. He handed the hoe back to Billy. "Got it?"

"I guess there is no point in saying *I don't get it,* is there?" replied Billy, scrunching up his face and rolling his eyes.

"No, William, there is no point to saying that," replied his father as he walked to the far side of the house.

Billy started to hoe. He pulled out roots. And he hoed and pulled and hoed and pulled. Finally, the wheelbarrow was full. Billy sighed, dropped his hoe, and wheeled the load over to the compost box beside the fence separating the Cooper property from The Glen. The fence was made of concrete with vertical slats that made it impossible to climb from one side to the other. He looked up at the maple tree on the other side of the fence. It was at the end of the boulevard that separated Maple Lane from the fence that separated The Glen from the freeway and the Cooper property. It was old. Not just really old, like Mrs. Cooper, but really, really old. It started from a seed long before the Cooper place even existed. *At least that is what everybody always said.* One of the branches was so humongous it reached right over the fence and right over the compost pile and right over the old garden shed and right over the raspberry patch at the end of the garden. Billy glanced quickly up at the spot where the branch went over the garden shed. That was a gang rule. Never look up at the maple tree when anyone not in the gang was around. Even if no one was near you, someone might be watching you and might follow your gaze to the branch that came within one meter of the garden shed roof. That was the way. That was the secret passage to the Cooper place. You could walk along the path that ran beside the fence and, when no one was looking, dart behind the maple tree and climb up into the branches. Once you were two meters from the ground you were invisible in the mass of gigantic green leaves. It was only a matter of walking along the giant branch and holding it up until you were above the garden shed. If you dropped straight down, you were out of sight of anyone in

The Glen.

Billy dumped the heap of roots and weeds into the compost box. He was about to turn back to the garden when a flash of sunlight caught his eye. He covered his face with his hand. Billy looked quickly around for his Dad. No one was in sight. He casually looked up at the branch above his head and followed it to the garden shed roof. He slowly turned his back on the shed and looked away from the fence separating the Cooper place from the Glen.

Billy spoke just above a whisper, "What do you want, Jackie?" He knew who was up in the maple tree. It was Jack Houston. AKA Jackie Spratt the Brat. The Spratt part came from the fact that he was skinny like the original Jack Spratt. You know—like the nursery rhyme—"Jack Spratt could eat no fat and his wife could eat no lean." The "Brat" part was because he was just so irritating. Jackie preferred to be known as Tinker because he liked to tinker with everything. Most of his toys were in various states of deconstruction. Jackie always said he took them apart in order to see how they might be "repurposed." He had *repurposed* his old baby monitor as a surveillance device to spy on his sister. Billy smiled to himself as he remembered the day she found it. Jackie got grounded for, what seemed like forever.

He continued, "I am not turning around so you can use that mirror to flash the sun in my eyes again. What are you doing up in the tree? You know you are not supposed to hang around in the tree. You might expose the secret passage. If that happens..." he paused, "well, you know what will happen."

"I was bored, and my mom was going to force me to do some awful chore, like clean the BBQ, or worse—clean my not-so-humble abode, AKA my *bedroom*," Jackie whispered from above. "You have no idea how the thought of that nauseates me. There are some seriously mutated flora and fauna under my bed that are best left undiscovered until they have reached the fossil stage of their evolution. So, I vacated the premises." He always spoke using big words. Jackie had a rule: Why use one word to express yourself when you could use three *and the bigger the better*. Billy hardly took any notice of it anymore except when "The Brat" used words he didn't know like flora and fauna.

"I know I am going to regret asking this, but here goes... What are flora and fauna?"

"Hah, I'm glad you asked," Jackie proclaimed proudly.

"Shhhh," whispered Billy. "My dad is around somewhere."

"Okay," Jackie whispered back. "The fauna would be my gerbil Mad Max who escaped from his "jail" last week and has been hiding out. He was probably joined by an arachnid or two, as well as maggots from a blue bottle. The flora was probably Neurospora crassa or Aspergillus nidulans—mold to you commoners, growing on pizza crust or various other pieces of midnight snack leftovers." He grinned.

"Yep! Sorry I asked," replied Billy. "Now go home."

"But I thought I would assist my best friend with his chores," Jackie said as his hands parted the leaves and he looked down at Billy. "On second thought, your chores seem to be worse than the ones I just escaped. I'll just come down and keep you company."

"You just want to watch me work," retorted Billy.

"That too," laughed Jackie.

"I'll see you at my house this afternoon. Remember the club meeting to discuss stuff. My dad will be gone to meet one of his new clients," Billy said as he picked up the wheelbarrow.

"OK. Are the plums ripe yet? Can we stuff ourselves? What about the cherries? I know the Braves make a raid every summer. Maybe we could check out what's ripe? What do you think, *William Earle*?" teased Jackie.

"We'll see, *James Percy*," said Billy smiling. "See you this afternoon." He knew Jackie hated his real name more than

William hated his. He pointed the wheelbarrow towards the garden as a rustle of leaves and a creak of a branch signaled Jackie's exit.

BUCKLES AND BONES

CHAPTER 2

Billy sighed and returned to his chore. *Hoe—pull—hoe—pull until the wheelbarrow's full.* Hey! thought Billy, *that rhymes.* He smiled and chanted to himself as he pushed the overloaded wheelbarrow towards the compost pile. Wheel. Dump. Wheel. Dump. Suddenly, the wheel hit a dip in the ground and he lost control of the full wheelbarrow. The whole load spilled three meters from the compost pile.

"Rats!" he cursed. *Wheel—dump—wheel—dump—avoid the nasty hidden bump!* He refilled the wheelbarrow with the weeds and roots and dumped them on the compost pile. "Gotta fix that hole," he mumbled to himself and grabbed the shovel leaning up against the shed. He scraped some dirt from the edge of the garden and put it in the hole. It was bigger than he thought. He poked the ground around the hole. There was not a lot of loose soil nearby, but he spotted a large rock that he could put in the hole and just fill around it. He wheeled the wheelbarrow over to the boulder and heaved it up inside.

He wheeled over to the hole, wrestled the boulder out of the wheelbarrow into his arms, and dropped it into the centre of the depression. As it hit the ground he heard a splintering sound and the rock sank practically out of sight. At the same instant something flew up into the air. Billy watched a dirty brass colored object, rectangular in shape, twist and spin in the sunlight, then drop with a plink on to the small section of the boulder sticking out of the ground. It bounced into the dirt. He reached for it. As his fingers curled around the brass object he leaned on the boulder. He heard another crack and the boulder slipped further into the hole, practically out of sight. Billy tried to catch his balance—both arms outstretched to break his fall—but fell forward into the dirt. What's happening? he thought.

His left hand still clutched the brass object while his right plunged deep into loose earth. He turned his head to the side, trying to avoid smashing his face into the top of the large dirt covered rock. He scrabbled with his empty right hand in an effort to stop himself from sinking further into the hole. His fingers curled around a long smooth object. He sputtered, spitting dirt out of his mouth, and rolled over out of the hole.

Lying on his back, breathing heavily for a moment, he lifted his arm to inspect what he held in his left hand. It was a belt buckle: an old, tarnished belt buckle with odd markings pressed into the brass on both sides. He slowly lifted his right arm. He was holding the skeletal remains of a human arm, from elbow to fingertip. It dangled before his eyes. The hand, still attached, flopped down at the wrist as if it were trying to grab on to Billy's face. He screamed and threw down the bones, quickly scrambling away from what he had just realized was a grave.

Billy stood and edged closer. Staring down at the bones in the shallow grave, he shuddered. A moment later, he heard his dad's truck pull into the driveway. (He'd gone to the building supply store to get some new pipe for the kitchen repairs.) Without even noticing that he had done it, Billy slipped the brass belt buckle into his jeans pocket. "Dad, Dad, DAD!" he yelled as he ran to the front yard. His father was just getting out of the truck. Billy continued to yell and point.

"What's the problem, William?" his father asked calmly. "You look like you've seen a ghost or one of those zombies from your video games."

"On the edge of the garden by the greenhouse—there is a … it's a … I dropped a rock—it broke open—I nearly fell in—I accidentally pulled something out—an arm—a hand—BONES!" He gasped for air and pointed to the backyard.

"Whoa. Slow down. What are you talking about?" His dad placed his hands on William's shoulders. "Shhhh … Start again, William. What happened?"

Billy breathed deep and let it out slowly. In a loud whisper he said, "There's a skeleton—an arm and a hand." He took another deep breath. "In the backyard, near the compost."

"A what? Are you sure?" his dad questioned.

"Yes," said Billy, "and it is human. Come and see." He rushed off in the direction of the backyard. He rounded the corner and looked back. He could not see his father, but the skeleton arm and hand were right where he had dropped it. The hand looked like it was trying to dig its way back underground to the safety of the grave. Billy ran back towards his father who was slowly walking in his direction. "Come on, Dad," Billy called. "Hurry up!"

"Well," his father drawled, "if it is a skeleton then it is not going anywhere. Are you sure it's not just some old dead cat?"

"It is not a cat," Billy shouted. "I've seen at least a

hundred episodes of CSI. I know human bones when I see them."

Billy's dad knelt down to examine the skeleton hand that seemed to be reaching down into the dirt depression surrounding the large boulder that Billy had dropped. He stood up and poked gingerly at the bones with his foot. Then he reached into his pocket and took out his cell phone. He dialed 911. "My name is Lawrence Braithwaite. I am at the old Cooper property. Yes, adjacent to the Beechwood Glen subdivision. Well, my son has found what appears to be part of a human skeleton. He was weeding in the garden. It looks old. Who should I call? Alright. How long? Fifteen minutes. Great. We'll be here. My number is 555-2385 ... Right."

He turned to Billy. "The police are coming. They will sort it out. How did you find this?"

Billy explained about the dumped wheelbarrow, the large boulder, falling into the grave, and pulling out the bones. He did not mention the brass buckle that felt warm in his pocket. In his mind, he watched it spinning in the air above the rock again, this time in slow motion. Flipping from side to side, each side overlapped the other, the design on it formed a picture that kind of looked like a house with a path leading away from it. A short whoop of a police siren brought his thoughts back to the present.

"That was sure fast," said Billy's father. "Just tell them what you told me, and all will be well."

They both turned and headed to the front of the house.

"What if they want to question me? Do you think they will want to take me *downtown*?" asked Billy.

"No, William, they won't take you downtown. You just found the bones, you didn't put them there. You are not a suspect; you are a witness. And anyway, the bones look really old," his father said as he walked towards the Royal Canadian Mounted Police officers getting out of their patrol car. He extended his hand and introduced himself. The police officers—one male and one female—nodded and shook his hand. "The grave is this way," he directed.

The three adults walked towards the backyard with Billy's dad taking the lead. Billy took up the rear. The police officers stopped and crouched down in front of the grave. One of them stood up and took a notebook out of her pocket. She turned to Billy and asked, "William, I understand you discovered these remains. Is this exactly how you found this site? With the arm bone protruding?"

Billy looked down at the arm bone and shuddered. "I accidentally pulled it out of the ground when I fell on the grave."

"What caused you to fall on the grave?" asked the police officer.

"I was reaching for the ..." Billy hesitated. Again, he felt the buckle warm in his pocket. "I was reaching to push the boulder. I put my weight on it, and it dropped down; I slipped and fell. My hand went into the hole. I tried to stop myself and grabbed ... *that*." He pointed at the skeleton arm and hand. "I pulled it out and dropped it there."

The other police officer was poking around the hole and pulled out a piece of board. He held it up and sniffed it. "I think it's pine and quite old. This is probably an old grave, but we better call Forensics just in case."

The shorter officer nodded, took out her radio, and walked a few meters away.

"Either way," her partner continued, "we'll need to move these bones somewhere else. I am going to have to ask you to step back while I create a site-perimeter. I'll need to get some yellow tape and support posts from the back of the patrol car." He began to walk away, then stopped, turning back toward Billy and his dad, he said, "Thanks for calling us."

Billy's dad nodded and followed him. The female police officer was talking on the radio. Billy was left staring at the grave. He put his hands in his pockets and felt the buckle. He saw it in his mind again, spinning in the air. He thought he could make out a picture as it spun. He heard a rustle of leaves and looked up expecting a gust of wind. Nothing moved. The hot sun reflecting off the roof of the garden shed wrinkled the air. He looked down at the grave and then heard the rustle of leaves again. Looking up, he saw Jackie parting the leaves he was hiding behind.

"Pssst," Jackie whispered. Billy quickly glanced at the police officer talking on the radio, then waved his hand, signaling Jackie to stay hidden.

Billy looked down at the grave and whispered just loud enough for Jackie to hear, "I'll meet you at my place later. Now get out of the tree."

The police officer turned and looked at Billy. "Pardon?" she said. "What's in the tree?" She looked up and Billy froze.

Billy turned quickly. "Nothing. Sorry. Just muttering to myself. I guess I'd better get back to weeding the garden."

"Well, no, you can't continue weeding the garden until this is settled. I bet that is good news." She smiled and moved towards the grave. "I wonder how old this is. I bet it is from the pioneering days. I think they used to mine something around here … silver maybe. I can't remember, but something like that. He will probably turn out to be an old miner. Anyway, we will find out soon enough."

The other officer and Billy's dad were walking back. They went to work cordoning off the area around the grave with yellow "Do Not Cross" tape. Billy watched and occasionally glanced up at the maple tree branches. Nothing moved. Jackie must have climbed back down. Billy breathed a sigh just as his father looked up.

"Well, William. It is your lucky day. I want to hang around here until the grave is removed, but I guess you can go visit your friends."

"Can I stay and watch?" asked Billy.

Billy's father turned to the male police officer. "May we both stay?"

"Sure, but there won't be much to see. And you'll have to watch from behind the tape, which will need to go all the way over there," he said, pointing to where the path narrowed as it rounded the house. He looked at Billy. "The forensic guys they will likely put up a tent to keep the scene as uncontaminated as possible. Sorry, but those are the rules. In fact, you had better move back now, son. You too, Mr. Braithwaite. We will let you know when we are finished."

"Can you give me a ride home then?" asked Billy.

Billy and his father walked around the house. They

didn't speak again until they were driving down the long driveway. Billy's father spoke first. "I guess we might as well go for a long lunch. Would you like that?"

"I'm not really hungry," said Billy.

"I guess finding old bones has put you off, eh?" teased Billy's father. He chuckled. "I'll drop you off at the house while I go get more of the plumbing supplies I need. We'll get back at it bright and early tomorrow. I'll pick up a few groceries, too. What do we need?"

"Some milk and bread and something for supper," said Billy listlessly. He was thinking about the grave and the buckle that seemed, once again, to grow warm in his pocket.

"How about we order take-out tonight?" his father said, pulling the pickup into the driveway.

"Great," said Billy as he jumped out. "See you later."

The truck reversed out of the driveway and drove off. Billy waited until he could no longer hear the rumble of his dad's old truck, and then he turned and sat on the porch to wait for Jackie. He had just sat down when Jackie poked his head around the corner of the house, startling Billy.

"Took you long enough!" Jackie said.

"I really wish you wouldn't sneak up on me like that," snapped Billy.

"Let's go. I figure we will be just in time to see the best part," said Jackie as moved towards the street.

"Where?" asked Billy

"*Where do you think!?* We gotta climb the old maple, so we can watch them dig up the grave. Maybe the old guy was murdered or something. He might have a hole in his skull where they hit him with a rock pick. Maybe the murderers dropped the weapon in the grave. Those cops will pick up the skull and the rock pick and it will fit exactly to the hole in the skull. I don't want to miss that. Let's go," huffed Jackie as he walked towards the street.

"Forget it, Jackie. Somebody would see us for sure. The secret passage would be compromised," said Billy. Thinking about what he had just said, he smiled. Compromised! *He was starting to sound like Jackie.* He knew a few big words, too. "Besides, they said they were going to put up a tent. There won't be anything to see."

"Shucks. I really wanted to watch the forensic guys do their thing. It's too early for the meeting. The Braves won't be there for at least a half hour," said Jackie, looking at his watch. "What do you want to do?"

"Dunno," mumbled Billy. He slipped the buckle out of his pocket and rubbed it against his jeans.

"What's that?" asked Jackie.

"Dunno."

"What do you mean, you don't know? Let me see it!" commanded Jackie.

"See," said Billy, holding the piece of brass up.

"Give it here!" said Jackie. "I want to hold it."

Billy looked at the buckle and ignored Jackie's demand. He slowly turned it over in his hands. The brass was tarnished and dull. He rubbed it again on his jeans in an attempt to shine it up. "It's got funny markings on both sides. I thought it was a picture when I first saw it, but it doesn't make any sense."

"Where did you get it?" asked Jackie.

"Found it," said Billy, "while I was digging in Mrs. Cooper's weed patch.

"Lemme see," insisted Jackie with his hand outstretched.

"Okay. But give it right back," replied Billy, cautiously handing over the buckle.

Jackie flipped the buckle over. "Looks old," he said. He spit on it and rubbed it with the edge of his T-shirt.

"Hey," yelled Billy. "That's disgusting." He grabbed the buckle and wiped it on his own T-shirt.

"It's just spit. It's got enzymes in it, and they can remove dirt and stuff. And anyway, I just wanted to see the detail. Give it back for a second!" demanded Jackie.

"OK, but don't spit on it. What the heck are enzymes?" asked Billy, handing the buckle back.

Jackie took the buckle and turned it slowly in his hands, inspecting it carefully. "Enzymes are proteins that catalyze chemical reactions," he replied absently, then breathed on the buckle and rubbed it again on his T-shirt.

"English, please!" retorted Billy.

"What?" Jackie said, flipping the buckle over and back a few times.

"Never mind, Einstein," Billy said sarcastically.

"Spit helps break down your food as you chew it, as well as provide lubrication for swallowing. It's good for cleaning stuff too," Jackie said, flipping the buckle back and forth. "It is definitely a picture of something. But what? Can I borrow it for a couple of days, so I can figure it out for you?"

"No. It's nothing. Just some doodles," said Billy, taking the buckle back from Jackie. He put it in his pocket. "What are we going to discuss at the meeting?"

"The guys will want to plan a sleep-out and cherry raid like last year. Boy, I never ate so many cherries in my whole life. I lived in the bathroom for two days. Boy, were those cherries ever good!" he added, smiling at the memory.

"Cherries won't be ripe for at least another couple of

weeks," Billy replied. "Let's go and meet the guys." They stood up and started down the sidewalk.

"Race you," said Jackie.

"Naw. We got twenty minutes to kill before they show up. I'm walking," said Billy as he placed one foot carefully in front of the other along the cracks in the sidewalk, as if he were on a tight rope.

Jackie fell in step behind him as they headed to the meeting of the Beechwood Braves.

THE
CLUB
MEETING

CHAPTER 3

The meeting always started with a roll call. Everyone was lined up with their backs against the fence at the end of Maple Lane. A grassy strip of land ran the length of the fence. All the roads that ran perpendicular to the fence ended at the edge of the grassy strip. It was no more than 10- meters wide. The old maple was at one end, just inside the fence. Billy knew who was there, but it was protocol to call out everyone's name. He liked to pretend he was looking at a list and reading the names. He would mix up the order so that no one knew who was next unless you were the last. Then you knew because there was no one else.

"Binky," he called.

"Here," Binky whispered.

"Binky," Billy called again. He had heard Anthony Berkowitz, AKA Binky, but he wanted to make him speak louder. Binky looked at the ground and grabbed onto the pouch he wore around his waist. The pouch hid a small stuffed animal that no one had really seen except Jackie. He had snuck a peek once when he was at Binky's house. Everyone knew it was there, though, and hence his nickname. Binky carried his binky with him at all times.

Jackie threw his hands in the air. "Oh, for fiddles sake, Bink, speak up."

"Here," said Binky. He had not spoken any louder than he had the first time, but Billy knew better than to push the issue.

"Mad Dog," he said.

"Here," said Maddox O'Hara. Maddox was a big boy with a large head of thick red hair and a face covered with freckles. The gang called him Mad Dog or Red Dog or sometimes just Dog. His nickname suggested he was tough, but Maddox was anything but tough. He liked animals, especially soft cuddly dogs, but he could never have one because his mom was allergic to just about everything.

"Petra," said Billy.

A tall girl standing in the middle of the group did a series of cartwheels around Billy and said, "Here, here, here, here" four times, one for each cartwheel. Her name was Elizabeth Petra Werner. Everybody called her Petra.

She hated Elizabeth and all the short forms like Beth and Lizzy or Liz.

"Sharming," said Billy.

"Present," said Sharming. His English accent was pronounced. So were his manners. They were both perfect. Devansh Sharma had recently moved into one of the older homes at the far end of Beechwood Glen. His family had moved from Mumbai the previous year. He was a small boy, but he was very smart—not smart like Jackie but smart like your teacher was smart. He knew lots of stuff, but he seldom said anything until he was asked. When he first joined the Braves, Petra called him Charming Sharming. The Sharming part stuck.

"Orph," said Billy.

"I am here," she said curtly, then continued, "Where else would I be? God, this taking attendance is majorly lame. All you have to do is look up and see that we are all here. I want to make a motion that we stop taking attendance. Any discussion?" She looked at everyone. No one said a word. "Great. There is no discussion, so let's vote. All those in favor of stopping this silly activity of taking roll call raise your right hand and say aye." She raised her hand and said, "Aye." No one said anything. They were all used to her antics. Her name was Sally-Anne Singleton. She was always staying at someone else's house, and Billy's sister called her Little Orphan Annie. The gang shortened it to Orph.

Billy shrugged his shoulders and said, "I call this meeting to order."

"Just a minute, Billy Boy. You seem to have forgotten something," said Jackie.

"What have I forgotten?"

"Well, from my perspective you seem to have committed a giant faux pas."

"A what?" asked Petra.

"I think he said giant foam pot," whispered Binky.

"An error. A social mistake that might cause embarrassment," corrected Sharming.

Billy spoke up. "Okay, Jackie, what did I do?"

"It was not what you did; it was what you neglected to do," said Jackie.

"What did I neglect to do?" Billy asked.

"I can't believe you didn't notice what you did not do." They all looked at him questioningly. "You were taking roll call ... and you seem to have ... forgotten ... something." They all looked at him again. Jackie waved his hands about in exasperation. "You did not call *my* name. I am part of this gang. A very important part, I might add, and I deserve the respect of being included when the roll is called."

"Sorry," said Billy before calling out, "Jackie?"

Jackie frowned. "I told you to call me Tinker. Everyone has a cool nickname, and I want to be called Tinker."

"Sorry. Tinker," said Billy.

Here," said Jackie.

They all sat down in a circle with Billy leaning against the concrete fence. "Right. We are all here, so let's open the floor to discussion. School has been out for a week now, and we still have no plans. Any suggestions?" asked Billy.

Jackie raised his hand but immediately started speaking. "Billy and I checked out the fruit trees at the Old Cooper place and nothing is ready yet. So, I thought we might get ourselves a clubhouse, like a real gang, instead of meeting here by the fence." He paused. "We could scrounge up some building materials. I know where there is a stack of old 2x4s."

Sharming raised his hand carefully and waited for Billy to acknowledge him. Billy nodded, and he spoke. "I like the idea of a secret clubhouse, but there is only one prob—"

Orph started talking. "Secret—a secret hideout. That would be *very* cool. I could, I mean, *we* could sleep in it and use it as our base for cherry raids."

"A clubhouse, not a hideout, and I doubt it would be secret," said Jackie.

"*Why not?* I like the idea of a secret place where we could meet," said Mad Dog. "We could store stuff in a secret hideout. I could hide my skateboard, so my creepy big brother can't steal it."

Petra did another series of cartwheels and spoke while she spun, "I don't know if my dad would let me."

Jackie was warming to the idea of a secret hideout as opposed to a clubhouse and burst out, "What part of secret do you *not* understand? If it were a *secret*, your dad would never know. *Geez.*"

Binky whispered something that Billy only half heard. Billy spoke to him, "Binky has something to say." He looked expectantly at Binky.

"I can get a big green tarp," he said.

"Good," said Billy. "We have some 2x4s and a tarp. What else would we need?"

"Plywood," said Mad Dog. "I think we might be able to borrow a couple of pieces from the recycle pile in my yard. No one would even notice"

"Now we are talking. But we have a problem," said Billy. He looked around at everyone, and they looked back expectantly. "Where can we build it? I know Beechwood like the back of my hand. The only place I can think of is the small wooded area behind Old Leach's house, but he would kick us out before we even started."

"That's a problem alright," said Maddox.

"I have to go soon. If I don't do my chores, my dad will be on my case. Everyone think about where we might build this *secret* hideout and scrounge up any building materials you can. We will meet here on Thursday," said Billy.

Everyone drifted away to their respective houses. Everyone except Petra. She cart-wheeled down the lawn. Jackie pulled Billy aside and whispered in his ear, "Wanna check out the grave? All we have to do is mosey on over to the maple, climb over and onto the roof. If no one is there, we could peek inside the tent. What do you think?"

"No way, too risky. My dad would kill me if we messed with a possible crime scene. Anyway, Dad is getting some takeout and I want to make sure it's pizza; otherwise, he will get Indian or Greek. Yeech. See you after work tomorrow."

Billy started to run home, leaving Jackie ambling along, kicking rocks on his way home. Suddenly, Jackie looked up and yelled in the direction of Billy's house, "I don't suppose you might consider inviting your best friend over for pizza!?" But Billy was gone.

a TUNNEL TO NOWHERE

CHAPTER 4

The next morning when they arrived at the Cooper place, Billy could see the tent still in the backyard, covering the old grave. It was wrapped in yellow police tape with the words *Do Not Cross* repeated along its length.

"Seems they haven't taken the skeleton away yet," noted Billy.

"They decided it was not a case of foul play, so they are leaving it in place until they can get someone from the university to check it out. That will happen sometime later in the week. The police asked me to keep an eye on the tent and make sure it was not disturbed." He looked at Billy. "I am delegating that responsibility to you. No one is to enter that tent and touch the bones. Are we clear?"

Billy knew what "are we clear" meant. "Yes, sir," he responded quickly. "No one is to go near the tent. I will let the Braves know."

"Especially Jack Houston," said his father. He let the name Houston hang in the air as if it had special meaning.

Billy understood what he meant. "I will make sure he doesn't disturb anything."

Billy was given a new job. His dad had to do a major repair on the kitchen pipes. Some of them were made of lead and lead was a huge health problem, especially when it was used in water pipes. It was poisonous. He had to tear out all the old pipes, replace them with copper, and use a solder that did not contain any lead.

"Why would they use lead if it was poisonous?" asked Billy.

"Guess they didn't think it could come out of the metal. I suppose it happens so slowly that nobody noticed. They also used it in some paints and kids got sick when they chewed on their painted toys. Lead gets into the environment and is ingested by animals as well. They get sick and die. We even used to use it in gasoline for our cars. Notice the gas pumps now say, "Unleaded." Interesting, huh?" His father smiled. "You need to know this stuff if you are going to be helping me."

"Yeah, I guess." Billy shrugged. "What do you want me to do?"

"You can start by taking out all that junk to the truck,

and then we have to clean down there," he said, pointing at the middle of the kitchen floor, then he handed Billy a pair of work gloves. "Use these."

Billy stood looking at the kitchen floor where his father had pointed. "Down where?" he asked.

"Down in the old cellar. Get this stuff cleaned up, and I will show you," replied his father.

Billy cleared up all the junk on the floor of the old kitchen. It was mostly bits of wood, plaster, and pipe that his dad had torn out the day before. He carried it to the truck. He knew better than to throw the stuff in the back of the truck. His dad had told him to put an old tarp in the back and then place the junk on the tarp. No throwing. Billy could hear his dad's favorite saying, *"Respect your tools and they will serve you well."*

Billy placed all the junk in the truck. "Dad, the truck is full," he announced.

"Good work. I'll take it to the Recycling Centre. I want you to go down there," he said, gesturing toward a trapdoor in the corner of the kitchen, "and clean out any junk that you find. I need the cellar cleared so I can fix these pipes from below. Stack the junk in the front yard, and I will make a second trip to the Recycling Centre. If you find anything valuable, you can keep it. There are some old stories about gold and silver being melted down in the cellar of the Cooper place. My grandfather used to tell me stories about a band of thieves that were never caught. They used to steal gold and silver from peoples' houses in town—and from the miners when they came back from the gold fields. They would melt it down and sell it." He laughed and wiped some of the sweat from his forehead with the back of his hand. "Mrs. Cooper says that those are old wives' tales. Her grandfather used to cast brass trinkets. She still has some of them. A seahorse and a unicorn, I think. They used to be on the mantle above the fireplace when I was a kid. Pretty cool stuff."

"I can have any gold that I find?" asked Billy. "Really?"

"Absolutely," said his father with a grin on his face as he left the house. He called back, "Get a move on. I'll be back in an hour or so. Oh, and you will need a light. I don't think there are any lights down there. You will find a flashlight in the tool box."

Billy cast his eyes to the outline of the trapdoor. Close to the wall was a hand grip that was used to open the wooden cover in the floor. "The Secret Door in the Floor" would make a great title, Billy thought. He had to remember it when school started. He could use it for a story.

He picked up the flashlight and pulled up the hinged

trapdoor. The door dropped open with a bang, and dust filled the air. Billy pointed the flashlight at the dust-filled darkness below. A steep set of wooden steps appeared in the beam of his flashlight. *Spooky,* he thought, and then, *Don't be stupid. Get down there and clean it up.*

He went down the steps backwards like he was climbing down a ladder, holding onto the handrail. He jumped onto the floor from the last two steps, turned around, and swept the flashlight over the room. It wasn't totally dark. There was a small, high window covered with boards. The light through the cracks caught the dust stirred up by his jump to the floor. He coughed and looked up at the opening at the top of the stairs, checking to make sure the door was still open. *Maybe that's why people called it a trapdoor—it trapped people in spooky cellars like this one.*

There wasn't much to pick up and take out to the tarp his father had left. It was mostly dust and spider webs. And even they looked abandoned. All the spiders were long gone, leaving only tattered webs behind. *What did that say about this place,* he wondered.

On one wall was a large metal hood that tapered to a pipe and went through the wall at its highest point. Below the hood was what looked like a barbecue pit filled with black clinkers or lava rocks. Billy leaned over, pointing the flashlight at the black surface. His foot stepped on something, but before he could lift it, a quick puff of air burst up from the black lava rocks, carrying dust with it. The dust filled his face and eyes; he coughed and stepped back, his heart pounding. He shone the flashlight at his feet and saw that he had stepped on a pedal of sorts. He gingerly stepped on the pedal again, and a puff of air came up, filling the flashlight beam with dust. Billy laughed and pressed the pedal again and again. "It pumps air into this big barbecue," he said out loud as he laughed and stepped on the pedal again.

He swept the flashlight around the room. Along the far wall was a wooden bench. It had small open boxes of sand, metal shapes, and various odd-looking tools strewn across it. Above that was a series of storage boxes set into the wall. They held more of the shaped metal objects, blocks of wax, and chunks of clay—long since hardened to rock. On the floor in one corner were some empty sacks that had once held sand, and some broken wooden boxes with a picture of an apple burned into one side. He picked up the pieces of boxes and carried them upstairs. *Gosh, I'll be finished in no time if this is all there is,* he thought as he climbed the stairs, went outside, and piled the trash on the tarp. He returned and picked up a sack, pausing when he heard a metallic tinkle. Something was inside. Reaching inside, he retrieved a fork and a small spoon. *Weird*, he thought, wondering why silverware would be in a sack. He put them on the bench with the other metal objects and carried the sacks up the ladder, adding them to the junk boards on the tarp. Just then he heard a truck. He looked up and saw that his dad had returned.

"What else is left down in the cellar?" his father asked as he got out of the truck and looked over the tarp pile.

"Not much," Billy replied. "Just some bits and pieces on the bench and in the wooden cubbies. Lots of weird stuff."

"What kind of weird stuff?" his father asked. "I have not been down there yet to explore. I only caught a glimpse from the trapdoor opening."

"There's a barbecue down there. It looks like a barbecue, anyway, but it's "built-in." It has a smoke hood and lava rocks. The same kind of rocks that we used to have in our old barbecue," he prattled, "and wax, and weird pieces of metal, and a funny thing that blows air right into the barbecue when you press on it."

"That must be the old forge," his father said, responding to Billy's puzzled expression.

"What's a forge?" asked Billy.

"Well..." he began slowly. "On second thought, why

don't we just go and check it out."

He grabbed trouble light and an extension cord. Lighting their way down, he then hung the bright light on a nail sticking out of an old beam.

Billy could see everything clearly.

"Yep, it's an old forge, and this is called the bellows. They would start a fire with coal in the fire pit here." His father pointed at the centre pit. "They pumped air into the fire with the bellows to add more oxygen and make the fire hot enough to melt metals like bronze and silver and even gold. Come to think of it, Mrs. Cooper had lots of metal trinkets and figurines. I bet they were cast in this room. They must have been made by her grandfather. We can ask her when she visits next month." He stopped and looked around. "Let's get to work. See those pipes up there?" he asked, pointing to the ceiling above the bench. "We have to get them out of there, so I can install new ones."

For the next two hours, Billy was running and fetching and holding anything his father asked him to fetch or hold. They stopped for lunch after the old pipes were out and the new ones in. After lunch, Billy's dad had to go across town to bid on his next job. He asked Billy to clean out all the wooden cubbies and gather all the bits and pieces and put them in a box for Mrs. Cooper to look through. Billy climbed up on the bench and started to empty each of the small cubbies. Spiders were his only concern. He shined the flashlight into each cubby before reaching in to collect the contents. He put all the metal pieces in one box and the wax carvings in another.

In one of the upper cubbies was a metal ring, like what you might see in the nose of a storybook bull. Billy smiled at that thought, then grabbed it, but it didn't move. One edge was stuck to the bottom of the cubby. He pulled as hard as he could, but the cubby was too high for him to put any real power into it. He climbed down, grabbed a thick block of wood from under the bench, and climbed back up and on top of the wooden block to have a better angle. Grasping the metal ring with both hands, he pulled.

For a moment the ring remained where it was, stuck in the bottom, but then it gave way and slowly came out of the cubby. There was a wire cable attached to the bottom of the ring that vanished down a small hole in the cubby. Billy gave it a strong tug, and suddenly he was falling over backwards. There was a rumble a creak and a whipping sound as the cable snapped tight. Then a crash and the sound of splintering wood as the box of metal trinkets was tipped onto the floor. Billy jerked to a stop. He was leaning backwards holding onto the ring with the cable stretching back into a hole in the cubby. Something else had happened as well. The left side of the shelf containing half of the cubbies had swung open, leaving a gaping black hole in the wall in front of Billy. He gasped and pulled himself upright. He could feel cool air rushing out of the hole into his face. He put his hand up to feel it and startled. There was blood on his hand. The sharp edge of the metal ring had cut into his fingers when the cable attached to it had become taut. Instinctively, he brought his cut hand to his mouth and sucked the blood to ease the pressure of the building pain. He brushed some dirt from his face and obliviously smeared blood on his cheek and forehead.

Billy climbed down off the bench. He sucked on his cut hand, never taking his eyes off the gaping hole in the wall. His heart had been jumping in his chest and was beginning to slow. He'd also been holding his breath. When his feet hit the floor, he sucked air into his lungs and glanced up at the trapdoor. He thought about his father who wouldn't be back for at least an hour. Now there was a hole in the wall, a huge, black, spider-filled hole in the wall above the bench.

Billy reached out and felt for the flashlight he'd left somewhere on the bench. For fear of what might crawl or leap out of it, he would not take his eyes from the hole in the wall. He took a deep breath and focused, trying to slow his pounding heart while searching for the light with his hands. If he glanced away from the hole, even for the nanosecond it would take to find the flashlight, a beast might leap from its prison, through the lattice of web right onto Billy Boy and do whatever it is that monsters from secret dark spider-filled holes in the wall do to children.

Billy's hand found the flashlight. His heart slowed a little. Turning the light on, he pointed it at the hole in the wall. His heart was nearing a normal pace, and he thought *Billy Boy, you are an idiot. There is nothing there. It's just a dirty old hole in the wall.* He laughed at his silliness and deliberately turned his back to the hole. Thinking better of it, he quickly spun back around, as if to catch whatever might be creeping out of the hole. Maybe he could freeze it, like in the game "Go – Go – Stop." If you saw someone move after you called "Stop" they were out of the game. If he caught the creature that was imprisoned in the black hole in his flashlight beam, he could freeze it mid-jump and survive the attack.

"Don't be a silly newt," he said out loud. The sound of his own voice seemed to calm his nerves. "Get up on that bench and look in there." He climbed up on the bench and stuck his flashlight through the spider webs. It was a small empty grotto-like cave. The floor of the cave was three stone steps down. Billy waved his flashlight in a circle to clear away the spider webs and give him a better view of the cave. There seemed to be nothing unusual: the floor was dirt; the walls were rock. Except his flashlight didn't illuminate a back wall.

Taking a deep breath, he stepped down to the cave's floor. He went three steps forward before he had to duck his head. The cave was like a funnel that narrowed down and to the left. He crouched and moved forward, holding the flashlight out in front like a light saber. *He would use it to slice through any monsters that might be hidden around the corner.*

He laughed out loud at his silliness. *An imaginary weapon to save him from the attack of an imaginary monster,* he thought as he crawled forward and poked his head around the corner. The beam of the flashlight slid over a wall of red brick. Billy turned and looked around. The cave was empty. He breathed in the cool air. "I wonder what's..." He stopped talking. He had heard something. He held his breath. *There!* He heard it again. He moved back toward the opening, trying to locate the direction of the sound. He heard a loud metal clank. It sounded like it was coming from the bricked-up wall. Billy turned and scrambled up onto the bench and out of the cave. His heart was beating like bongo drums in his chest. He reached over and pushed on the wall of cubbies to close-up the cave. The metal ring on the end of the cable slithered back into the cubby that concealed it and the wall closed. The sound did not. There was a loud crash, but it came from upstairs. *Did this cave play sound tricks?* Billy breathed deep.

"William—are you still down there?" he heard his father yell from the kitchen above the cellar. "I need a little help here. My meeting was cancelled, so I bought some of the materials we need."

Billy climbed the wooden stair ladder and poked his head out of the trapdoor.

"There you are. Help me unload the truck," said Billy's father. He looked at Billy's face and reached out, grabbing him by the shoulders. "What happened to you? You've got blood all over your face."

"It's nothing," replied Billy, realizing the sound he had heard was his father dropping bags of pipe fittings on the floor of the kitchen above. The sound must have echoed off the brick wall. He breathed out slowly. "I'll get what's left in the truck."

He left the room not knowing why he didn't tell his father about the secret wall of cubbies and the empty cave.

TREE FORT

Billy cleaned up all the junk in the kitchen—and below the kitchen. His father went about changing the pipes, and Billy was reassigned to the garden. He had to start a new compost pile closer the edge of the property because the police tent was still in place. Billy hoed and hoed. His thoughts wandered from the secret cave below the Cooper house to possible locations for the secret hideout. Once his wheelbarrow was filled, he pushed it to the base of the large cedar trees at the edge of the property where he dumped it. The sun was almost at its highest point. Billy was sweating. He cursed himself for forgetting to bring water. He knew that his father had shut off the water to the Cooper place while he replaced the pipes. There was no water to be had.

Billy sat down with his back to the trunk of the largest cedar tree. Tilting his head, he stared up the trunk of the tree. The branches at the back swayed down, almost touching the ground. Suddenly, he had an idea and jumped to his feet. Walking around the tree, ducking under the low branches, he looked up again. He was considering a tree house. To his surprise, he found a series of boards nailed to the back of the tree trunk. The first few were rotten and barely holding on, but as he looked higher he could see many more steps that might still hold his weight. About halfway up the tree he spotted the remains of a platform. Billy jumped up in an effort to grab on to one of the more solid boards, but they were just too high. He stopped and looked at the large bent branches. He walked over to where a large one curved down from the tree trunk. Standing on its lowest point, he reached up and grabbed a higher branch. Pausing to steady himself, he slowly walked up the branch until he reached the trunk. Then he climbed onto one of the boards that was part of the makeshift ladder leading up to the platform.

He looked over at the house. His father was still inside. He started to climb, testing each step before putting his full weight on it. He managed to climb six steps up the tree. The seventh step came away in his hand when he reached up to grab it. This was as far as he could safely go. Examining the pattern of branches, he realized that he could abandon the steps and use the branches to climb up to the platform. There was an opening in the floor above him right next to the trunk. He planned his ascent carefully, stepping from branch to branch. At one point, he had to go all the way around the tree to reach a secure handhold. Finally, he poked his head through the hole in the platform that surrounded the tree. It was not designed as a tree house, more like a platform used to observe the surrounding area. He stepped onto the platform, holding onto a couple of branches that had been notched for hand holds. He imagined the floor he was standing on collapsing and sending him tumbling to the ground. He shook his head; the result of such a fall would be very unpleasant to say the least. Gingerly, he jumped up and down to test the boards. They seemed to be solid. There were large galvanized steel cables snaking around the tree supporting the main platform. The cables had been attached so that they could move with the tree as it grew. He relaxed as he looked around. This was some sort of lookout, and it was built to last. Some of the railing was rotten, but that could be fixed. He imagined some walls and a roof. That would make it a real hideout.

Billy sucked in his breath. He could see the entire Beechwood Glen, down the freeway in both directions, the forested median that separated the freeway, and even most of the Cornborough Estates on the other side of the freeway. His mind was racing. The gang would love this. He glanced back at the Cooper house. His dad was coming out the front door and heading to his truck.

"Crap," he muttered and started to climb down. He was much less careful and nearly fell when he put his foot on one of the rotten steps. It broke free and tumbled to the ground. It fell on the back side of the tree. His dad did not see the board fall, but he heard it and turned to stare at the backyard. Fortunately, he did not see Billy. He glanced towards the shed and the police tent and then back at the garden. Billy was almost to the ground when his dad called out his name. Billy quickly brushed himself off and stepped from behind the tree. He reached down and pretended to zip up his fly.

"Oh, there you are. I thought I heard something fall. Are you okay?"

"Yeah," said Billy, "I just had to go, so I stepped behind the tree."

His dad looked at the garden. "Slow progress, eh?"

"It takes forever to chop out all the roots."

"Yeah, I know. Lucky you have all summer to get the job done." He grinned. "Hungry?"

"Starving—and thirsty."

"Last night I bought a package of sliced ham and some wraps. Let's go home and make some lunch." He turned and headed to the truck.

Billy followed, but he was not thinking about food. The possibilities of the platform in the cedar tree becoming a perfect secret hideout ignited his imagination.

Later that afternoon, Billy completed weeding a two-meter section of the garden. He took the wheelbarrow over to the shed and leaned it up against the wall. He had to go around the police tape, and he was now standing on the back side of the tent. On an urge, he reached down and lifted the edge of the tent and peeked inside. The walls and ceiling of the tent were white, and the bright sun outside made the inside glow with bright light. The side he lifted was closest to the grave. He could see the white edge of something that was half-covered with dirt. It was one of the bones. He reran the scene of falling into the grave in his mind and realized that the white patch he was looking at was a section of the skeleton's skull. It was in the right place to be the skull—unless the body had been chopped up before being buried. Billy's imagination was suddenly off to the races. His head filled with questions he wanted answered. Who was this man? How did he die? When did he die? Was it a violent death? Why was the grave not marked? Maybe Mrs. Cooper knew who he was. Maybe it wasn't even a male.

He felt the shape of the buckle in his jeans pocket. He pulled it out and looked at it. It was shiny, clean, and warm. He slipped it back inside his jeans just as the kitchen door slammed. He quickly dropped the edge of the tent, brushed off the dirt on the knees of his jeans, and stepped from behind the tent. Walking straight back to the garden, he picked up the hoe he had left there.

On his way back to the shed, his father called out, "Let's call it a day, William. You want to stop for an ice cream on the way home? I could really use one."

"Sounds good," said Billy as he jogged to the truck. He was pushing all the thoughts of the grave and what he had done out of his mind. If his father knew he would not be happy. If Billy looked or felt guilty, his father might suspect. It was safer not to think about it at all.

SCROUNGE AND SMUGGLE

CHAPTER 6

Billy was licking a huge chocolate ice cream cone as the cool air from the open truck window blew his hair into his face. The cone melted faster than he could lick. It dripped onto this shirt and down his chin.

His dad looked over at him and started to laugh. "Close the window and it won't melt so fast," he said.

Billy tried to turn the stiff window handle. That turned out to be a bad idea. Once he took his eyes off the cone, he did not notice that the cone was no longer upright. He felt more ice cream drip onto his shirt. He glanced back at the cone just in time to save the entire glob of half-melted ice cream from falling into his lap. "Oh, crap," he said.

"If your mother was here she would tell you to watch your language but, by the looks of you, I think it was appropriate." He pulled into the driveway. "Go in and get cleaned up. I have to head over to Rona to pick up a couple things I couldn't find in town earlier. Mrs. Cooper won't be here until late September, but we have a lot of work to do to get that place livable."

"We? Dad, it's summertime. I'm just a kid."

"Yeah, just a kid that wants a very expensive portable game console. I am calculating your time. I'll tell you when you've earned it. I think you have just enough time to work off half the cost by your birthday in August. I will spring for the other half." Billy rolled his eyes. "Don't compare yourself to other kids that get everything just handed to them. I am equipping you with advantages that they will never have. You will be able to do practical work, and they will have to hire someone else to do it for them. That is my gift to you."

"Yes, Dad." Billy opened the truck door, still balancing what was left of the ice cream cone. He could feel the cold chocolate sweetness run down his arm and he knew there was no point in arguing. He turned back to his father, "I'm going to get cleaned up and then head over to Jackie's to play on his game console. Are you making dinner?"

"No, you are. I want you to make a meat-loaf like I taught you. All the fixings are in the refrigerator. Have it ready by 6:00. Oh, and toss a couple of potatoes in the oven with it. We can have that and some sliced tomatoes.

I saw a couple of ripe ones in your mother's garden."

Billy nodded and licked the stub of the ice cream cone, then he had an idea. "Hey, Dad. The last time I was at Rona I noticed a sign over a pile of old pallets that said they were free for the taking. Do you think you might toss six of them in the back of the truck? Me and the Braves want to build a clubhouse, and they would work well for the walls."

"The Braves and I," he corrected, "and yes, I will, if there are any there."

Billy watched his father drive away, then he headed into the house to clean up. Figuring he had at least two-hours before he had to start dinner, he put on a clean T-shirt and headed over to Jackie's house. He had gotten into the habit of taking different routes through the Beechwood complex. Back alleys were always good when scrounging for stuff. The pallets would be a real benefit. The Braves could use them as they were or take them apart and use the boards. Many of the pallets came from overseas countries and they were made of weird hardwoods. They would be perfect when it came to building the new steps up the back of the cedar tree.

There was nothing of use today along his route. He climbed onto the back porch of Jackie's house and knocked on the door. No one came to open it, but he heard Jackie's mother shout, "He's in his room doing something weird. Go on up, William."

Billy opened the door. Jackie's mom was a friend of his mother and hence called him William. There was no point in correcting her. To her he was William and that was that. He walked through the kitchen and up the stairs. He approached Jackie's door. He didn't knock. He formed his hand into a claw and scratched down the door three times as if he was one of the monsters in the horror movies. He heard Jackie's voice from the other side. "Come on in, Billy Boy."

He opened the door, stepped inside, and closed the door behind him. The door scratch was kinda like their password. If someone knocked it would give Jackie time to hide whatever he was secretly working on. He worked on his bed and had a blanket ready to throw over and conceal it all from unwanted visitors like his mom or his sister. There were always some dirty clothes around that he would toss on top to cover any random bumps and make anyone less likely to touch the mess. He'd learned the hard way. Last Halloween he'd found a bunch of old fireworks hidden in the garage. They were really old. Jackie had taken them apart and removed all of the gun powder. His plan was to make a bomb big enough to blow up something huge. He was in the middle of unwrapping a bunch of Roman candles when his dad had knocked on his door. Jackie was expecting Billy. He said, "Come on in, Billy."

His dad opened the door and saw all the fireworks. Everything hit the fan, so to speak. His dad took and destroyed all the fireworks while his mom railed at his dad for leaving them accessible for children to get into. Ever since then, the new protocols were in place. Claw the door three times as if you were Freddie Kruger and Jackie need not secure whatever he was working on.

Billy looked at the bed. It was covered in wires. On his desk was a small baby monitor. "Whatcha building, Dr. Strange?"

"Billy, am I glad to see you. Things have gone to caca. My whole summer might be ruined unless I do something," said Jackie.

"What?" said Billy.

Jackie walked over to his bedroom window, pulled the curtain aside and peeked out. "Look," he pointed.

Billy walked to the window and looked out. In the yard next door were two kids about his age playing on a slip-n-slide. One was a girl and one was a boy. They looked very much alike. "So?" said Billy.

"In case you didn't notice, they are right across the fence. They are here for the summer. They are incredibly irritating. They are twins which makes it even more irritating. And, worst of all, my mother said *I have to* entertain them all summer and be their friend. Just saying it makes me gag."

"Oh," said Billy.

"Oh. That is all you have to say, OH! I am at their beck and call. If they want to do something I am supposed to be their guide—slave is more like it."

"What are you going to do? We have plans. The Braves have plans."

"I'm glad you asked. I'm setting up a surveillance system that will tell me when they are coming over here, so I will have time to, as the Brits say, *scarper*."

"What?"

"Scarper, scram, vamoose, take a powder, vacate, bail, evacuate."

"Oh, I get it. Whenever they want you to do something with them, this will provide an early warning system, so you can show up at my place or end up watching me work from the maple tree." Billy pointed at the camera. "What's all this other stuff for?"

"I am extending the power line, so I can mount it under the eve out there," he pointed at the window, "and run the power from here. I have one of my mom's old cell phones that will connect to it via Wi-Fi. The camera has motion detection. It starts recording when someone moves towards the gate between the properties. They will come that way. I won't get a lot of time, but I will be warned."

Billy looked out the window again. "They don't look as bad as you are making out. What are their names?"

"Get this, Jimmy and Joanie. Who would name their kids Jimmy and Joanie? Joanie is the girl and she is especially painful. She is always smiling at me, as if I'm a new toy. She says things like, 'What would you like to do today, Jackie?'"

"What's so bad about that?"

"It's the way she says it – all sweet and sticky. Yeech."

"I think you are overreacting. On a different topic, I got my dad to check out the old pallets at Rona. He's gonna bring some home. I figured we could use the lumber."

"Cool."

"I found the perfect spot for our hideout today."

"Where?"

"At the back of the Cooper property there is an old observation platform up in the cedar tree. It needs some work, but I think we can make it into the coolest hideout ever."

"Great," he said. He was not really listening. He picked up a screw gun and fitted the bit. He pulled the trigger and the gun whirred.

Billy continued, "I'm just gonna need the Braves to help me get the stuff to the base of the secret passage. Once there, we can use a rope to get them to the other side of the fence. I want you to figure out a way to get materials over the fence and up the cedar tree. We will need some pulleys and some good rope. Any ideas?"

Jackie didn't answer. He peeked out the curtain again. "They've gone inside. Now's the time." He opened the curtains and the window. "I'm going to step out onto the roof with the camera and this screw gun." He held it up. "I'll screw the camera to the eve, plug it in, and point it at the gate."

"What do you need me for?"

Jackie picked up a man's belt from the floor and looped it through the one already around his waist. "You are going to hold onto the other end of this." He flapped the leather belt in front of Billy. "Got it?"

"Got it," replied Billy. "I won't let you fall."

A few minutes later the camera was mounted. Jackie

climbed back through the window and became occupied with connecting the phone via Wi-Fi.

"I need to get going. See you later," Billy said. Jackie nodded, still distracted. Billy headed home, his thoughts filled with possibilities of a summer with a secret hideout up a huge old cedar tree.

THE GARDEN SHED STORAGE

The pallets were in his father's truck. There were six of them in almost perfect condition. They were still on the truck when Billy and his father arrived at the Cooper place the next day. His father got out of the truck and noticed that they were still in the back. "Darn, I meant to take those out. Where do you want them? We can drop them off on our way home."

Billy had been trying to figure out where he was going to store them. The Braves needed them right where he was, and here they were. He took a shot, "Can we store them here for a while—until we decide where we're going to build our clubhouse?" Billy felt that this was not really a lie because they hadn't decided where they were building a clubhouse. They had decided that they were building a secret hideout.

"No problem, but you have to be responsible for taking

them off the truck," he said and added, "On your own time. They had better not still be here when it is time for you to go back to school."

"The Braves and I will deal with them. Thanks, Dad." He had solved a huge problem. All he had to do now was get them off the truck. "I'll do it now in case you have to pick something up. I'll make up the time."

His father nodded, already thinking of his next job.

Billy hauled the pallets to the back of the garden shed and leaned them up against the wall. He grabbed the hoe and dropped it in the wheelbarrow, then headed over to the garden patch. He hoed and hoed and wheeled and wheeled until lunch time, all the while planning the next steps to repairing the platform in the cedar tree. He could see it all in his mind. To make it real, he would have to take each of the pallets apart. That would be the first task. He would need all the Braves to help him. Once that was done, he needed to replace and repair the steps that went up the back of the tree. His father's words rang in his head, "Safety First – Speed Second." He always said it before any job. Billy thought of Binky trying to climb the steps up to the hideout. That might be a problem. They needed to make the climb much safer. Billy planned to set a series of pitons into the tree just like rock climbers did, so they would be able to clip onto the pitons as they climbed. If someone slipped, the safety rope would stop them from falling. He liked the idea. If anyone got hurt, then the whole secret jig would be up.

The more he planned, the longer the list of materials got. After dumping a load of roots beside the pallets, he went into the garden shed, looking for a place to store all the tools and materials required. The garden shed would be perfect. His dad had never even stepped inside, so he figured it would be safe enough, especially under a tarp. Looking around, he saw a small workbench at one end. There were no tools except a can of very rusty nails and a miner's rock pick. There was a carpenter's pencil, and pad of ancient paper, yellow and curled. Billy started a list:

screw gun
long screws
hammer
nails
rope
screw-in eye lags, as pitons
clips to use as carabineers and a safety belt

The wood pieces would be salvaged from the pallets— they'd need a pry bar for that. Once they had all of this, they could safely travel up and down the cedar tree to the platform. After that, the real construction would begin.

He hoped that Jackie could come up with an elevator system to get the materials up to the platform. He also hoped Jackie would keep the design simple, so they could actually build it. Jackie had a tendency to get a little "sophisticated." Billy did not want something that would be impossible to build, just something to ease the amount of work required to get boards and other materials up to the platform, especially heavy stuff.

Billy went to the house to check in with his dad. He found him lying on the kitchen floor with his head in the cupboard under the sink. Smoke from the propane torch was curling out of the opening. "Dad, it is lunch time."

"I'll be out in a minute. I just have to finish soldering this pipe."

Billy heard the torch light up and saw more smoke. "I'll get the cooler," he said and walked out to the truck. He flipped back the seat, grabbed the cooler, and was about to flip the seat back into place when he saw a can of large metal lag-eye screws. They were rusty but still good. He was sure his dad had forgotten all about them, so he grabbed the can, ran back to the garden shed and put them on the workbench. They would work for the pitons, and also might come in handy for whatever elevator system

Jackie created. Billy ran back and carried the lunch cooler into the house just as his dad was climbing out from under the sink. They sat and ate leftover meatloaf sandwiches.

"William, this is great meatloaf. You changed the recipe somehow. What did you do?"

William beamed. "There was no ketchup, so I used a bunch of other stuff I found. There was some teriyaki sauce and some Worcestershire stuff. I put that in along with some of the grated cheese."

"Well, it is even more delicious cold. You realize that you are now in charge of meatloaf dinners from now on. That's what happens when you get good at something. You become the go-to guy. Congratulations," he said.

Billy made a face. He did not want to be good at making meatloaf.

His father laughed.

Billy decided he would take advantage of his father's good humor. "Hey, Dad, do you think I could use your battery screwdriver to build the clubhouse?"

"Boy, this is your day. I just bought a new driver. You can have the old one. Its battery is not great, but I think it will work for you. It's on the counter over there." He pointed to a dirty, dinged-up screwdriver sitting on the counter across the room.

"Fantastic," said Billy. Grabbing it, he pressed the trigger. The screwdriver whirred.

"The charger is in the tool box. Grab it, too, before I take the tool box." Billy nodded. "Let's get back to it." His father stood, slipped on his gloves, and crawled back under the sink.

Billy took the screwdriver and charger out to the garden shed and plugged it in to charge the battery. He looked around and nodded. Things were coming together.

He went back to work. Hoe, pull, and wheel—hoe, pull, and wheel filled the remainder of the day. Billy was nearly half done. If he worked hard he could get it all done quickly enough to give him time to work on the hideout. He dropped the hoe and went to re-inspect the wooden steps at the back of the cedar tree. They had been inset into the trunk when they were originally installed. It would be a simple matter of knocking the rotten ones off, hammering in the old nails and screwing a new cleat in its place. He could inset one of the hooks a metre above the cleat, and he could clip onto that as he climbed and replaced cleats. It would be like climbing a mountain in preparation for the rest of the Braves.

Billy returned to the shed and decided that he would use it for a shop. If they worked inside the shed, then they could keep away from any peering eyes. He hefted one of the pallets and corner-walked it into the shed. He let it fall to the floor. It hit with a resounding boom that seemed to echo inside the shed, like he had banged on a big drum.

Billy examined the floor of the shed. It was constructed of old planks worn down from many years of footfall. He picked the pallet up again and looked under it. Nothing seemed out of the ordinary, so he dropped it again. The echoing boom filled the room along with a plume of dust. Once again Billy picked up the pallet and flipped it to the side. This time there was only a dull thud when it hit the floor. He jumped on the floor where the pallet hit, and a deep echo filled the room. The floor sounded hollow under a section. Billy grabbed the old rock pick from the workbench, got down on his hands and knees, and started to tap the floor. He discovered an area about one-metre square that created a consistent echo. He looked for the edge of a trapdoor. *There should also be something like a hinge,* he thought, but there was nothing. The boards just followed a seemingly random pattern. He shook his head. Maybe he was just letting his imagination get the best of him. After finding the hidden cavern with the bricked-up exit in the cellar of the house, he just figured that there must be something behind it. It would be pretty strange to brick something up for no reason. Maybe it led to the shed and came up inside. Maybe. Or maybe not.

Billy went out and walked around the perimeter of the shed, all the while staring at the foundation. Maybe there was a way into the underground tunnel from the outside. He found nothing. Returning to the shed and looking at the floor again, he could see nothing that might suggest a way down. If he had to chop or cut his way in, then there was probably nothing there. Just a hole in the ground. The last hole in the ground contained a body; an old skeleton that had not had any flesh on it in at least a hundred years. Billy mumbled aloud, "Well, Billy Boy, you are being really silly again. There is nothing here, and this shed will be a great workshop."

"William, where are you? It is time to go," called his father.

Billy set the old rock pick on the bench and shouted back, "Coming." He left the shed and walked around the police-taped tent. "I'm here."

His father was standing in the garden inspecting Billy's work. "This looks good. You will be finished sooner than I expected. I will have to find you a new job pretty soon." He grinned.

Billy whined, "Daaaad."

THE GANG

CHAPTER 8

After dinner and dishes, Billy ran out to see if any of the gang was hanging about on the boulevard. Mad Dog and Petra were tossing a Frisbee with Binky in between trying to intercept it. Sharming and Orph were playing rock-paper-scissors. It appeared as if Orph was losing every game.

As Billy approached, Orph stood up and shouted, "You have to be cheating. No one could beat me this many times in a row!"

"I am not cheating. I have never cheated. That would be very *ungentlemanly*. I told you that you have a *tell*," responded Sharming.

"Have a *tell?* I am not telling you anything. Do you think I'm stupid or something? I *know* you are cheating."

Whenever Sharming got stressed his English accent became more pronounced. "I am not *cheating*. I am simply reading you during the three-count." Billy approached and sat beside Sharming. "Tell her I am not cheating, Billy. She simply telegraphs what she is going to choose, and so I choose whatever will beat her."

"Like I said, he is *cheating*," said Orph. She crossed her arms and plunked down in the grass.

"Let me show you," said Sharming. He looked at Orph. "Are you ready?" Orph nodded and they began to count to three. Orph's hand became flat like paper and Sharming's hand became scissors.

Crap!" Orph shouted, "See. He *has* to be cheating."

"Do you want me to show you your *tells*?" Sharming asked.

"What are *tells*?"

"It is when you do something with your body just before you choose whatever you are going to choose. When you bite your bottom lip on the left side of your mouth you are going to choose paper. When you stick your tongue out and touch your top lip you are going to choose rock and when you puff out your cheeks you will pick scissors. It is as simple as that."

"Crap. It is still cheating! You should have told me before you beat me a zillion times in a row. *I am never playing this game again.*"

"Now that you know, you can use that to your advantage and change your tell when it is important for you to win."

"Cripes, it's always important for me to win," said Orph.

Just then the Frisbee sailed and landed right in front of them. The rest of the Braves came running over. Billy asked them to sit. He wanted to tell them about the plans he had for the hideout. He was about to start when he noticed Jackie running towards the group. He slid to the ground and tried to hide behind Mad Dog. "Hide me."

It was too late. They all heard a voice and then saw the twins run out onto the grass. "He's over here," said the girl. Jimmy and Joanie ran up to the group. They stared at Jackie. "If I didn't know better I would say that you were trying to ditch us. Were you trying to ditch us, Jackie?" Jackie shrugged his shoulders, flopped down on the grass, and stared at the sky. "Cause if you were I would have to tell your mother and I don't think she would be happy."

Jackie sat up. "I was not trying to ditch you. I was simply leading you here, so I could introduce you to my friends. This here is Petra, Maddox, Anthony, William, Devansh and Sally-Anne. Guys, say hi to Joanie and Jimmy. They are visiting their grandparents and live in the house right behind mine."

Everyone said hi to the twins. This was followed by an

awkward silence that was broken by Joanie. "What are you guys up to?"

"We're not up to anything. The guys are just hanging out," said Jackie. "I was late, and they are probably heading home. Isn't that right, William?"

"Yeah," agreed Billy. Then he remembered their code for *meet at the maple tree as soon as you can.* "My dad wants me home. I have to work at the *Cooper Place* tomorrow and he wants to tell me what I am supposed to do. Catch you guys later." *Cooper Place* was the signal to pretend to go home, and then meet at the back of the maple tree just at dark.

Petra picked up on it first, "Yeah, me too. Come on, Maddox and Anthony. I will walk you home." Maddox nodded.

But Anthony did not even recognize his own name. He started talking, "My mom said I didn't have to be home until it was nearly dar—"

Petra grabbed his arm and pulled him toward her. "Not what she told *me*. She said I was to have you home before eight, and it is nearly that now. Come on." She grabbed one arm and Mad Dog grabbed the other. They practically lifted him off his feet and across the grass. Binky thought it was a game and went along willingly.

Orph and Sharming looked at each other. "Come on, Orph, I mean, Sally-Anne. I will show you how to use "tells" to your own advantage." Orph smiled a fake smile at Joanie and said, "Got to go."

Only Billy and Jackie remained. Billy started to walk away with a nod at Joanie. "Nice meeting you," he said.

Jimmy spoke for the first time. It was obvious that Joanie was the dominant one, but he turned to Billy, "Maybe I could get together with you sometime and hang out?"

"You mean WE, don't you?" interjected Joanie.

"Yeah, we could all get together."

"Sure. I guess. Sometime when I am not working. I have to work for my dad all summer."

Jackie spoke, "See you sometime when you get a few free minutes from working. Okay, William?"

Billy nodded. He was irritated that Jackie kept using his full name. "I have to go home, too. See you later." He and Billy walked off in different directions. Joanie and Jimmy followed Jackie. The last thing that Billy heard was Joanie telling Jackie that he had nice friends.

An hour later, Billy was walking toward the Maple Tree. The path had been well thought out. Each leg of the trip was designed so that only a select few places in Beechwood Park could see a person as he approached the tree. You had to start by walking with your head bowed along the hedge that ran beside the Fitzwilliam's and then dash across the open space of their driveway. From there, you were to walk casually along the road until you reached the low hedge on the other side. After a quick check to see if anyone was watching, you had to jump the hedge and crouch down behind it. Then you had to crawl along the hedge until you were at the concrete fence that ran beside the Cooper place. Once there, you had about a five-meter dash to the huge and gnarled tree trunk. From the back side of the tree trunk you could climb up into the branches and remain invisible.

Once he got to the back of the tree, he quickly climbed up. He could not really see anyone else, but he heard Orph. "It's about time. Everyone is here except Binky. His mom told him it was too late to go out with the gang. He made me promise to tell him everything that happens." Billy climbed up, and soon his light adjusted eyes could see the whole gang, minus Binky, sitting on one large branch.

"Glad you are all here. I have an announcement to make," said Billy. Everyone looked at him. "I have found the perfect spot for our secret hideout." He paused to see that everyone was staring with rapt anticipation. "It will require a lot of work but, believe me, it will be worth it."

Orph burst in, "Where?"

Billy looked around and slowly parted the leaves of the maple tree. The sun had just set, and the western sky was pink. You could see the copse of cedar trees at the back of the Cooper property silhouetted against the fuchsia sunset. "There, up in the largest cedar tree."

"I think you are dreaming, Billy Boy," said Jackie.

"I agree," said Sharming. "It would be very difficult to design and build a platform up that tree."

"That's the best part. We won't have to build it because *it's already there!* There are cleats on the tree leading up to it, like treads on a ladder. They need repair, but it's something I think we can do. I have already started collecting lumber and tools to do the job." He sat back and waited.

Mad Dog spoke first. "Who built it?"

Billy shrugged. "I think it was built a long time ago, before the freeway. It was built to last. It seems to be some sort of lookout because you can see all the way to Cornborough Estates and beyond."

Jackie jumped up from his crouching position on the branch and nearly slipped and fell. "Let's go and see it now."

"Not now. It's too dark. One thing you guys have to understand is that to keep this secret we must take care at all times. It's near the Cooper property. The house will be empty the whole summer, but my dad will be there a lot, so we can only work after 5 when he is gone."

"And on weekends," piped in Orph.

"Right. Tomorrow is Friday. I have to work tomorrow. On Saturday we can all go over and have a look," said Billy. They all agreed to meet in the maple tree on Saturday at 9:00 a.m. They left the maple tree one at a time.

Billy and Jackie were left in the tree. They both sat and waited for Petra to get past the Fitzwilliam's house. Jackie looked at Billy and raised his eyebrows. Billy knew what was coming next. Jackie wanted to climb up the tree right now. "No way. We are not going to risk it. You will just have to wait."

"Okay, okay. In that case I am going first. See you tomorrow."

"I have to work tomorrow," said Billy.

"I know," replied Jackie. He slipped down out of the tree and was gone.

Billy sat in the leaves for a few minutes. He reflected on the fact he was not being truthful with his dad. He shook his head, pushed the thought aside, and climbed down the tree.

EVERYBODY GETS A PEEK

The next morning Billy hoed and wheeled. It was surprisingly painless because his thoughts were running wild. He was trying to make sense of everything he had discovered at the old Cooper place: the secret passage from the cellar of the house to a bricked up underground passage; the skeleton buried in the backyard; and the platform in the cedar tree. It all kept running around in his head. They must be connected in some way. He felt for the brass belt buckle in his pocket. He took it out and looked at it more carefully. It was a curved rectangular piece of brass. On both sides were stripes of detail pressed into the surface. The stripes containing markings were offset. The corresponding reverse stripe was blank. In the middle of the top and bottom edges was a small hole. On the sides were sections where the belt might pass through. These seemed to have worn very thin, and the leather that used to attach to them must have long since rotted away.

Billy looked at the holes at the top and bottom of the belt buckle and remembered the day he fell into the grave. He could clearly see the buckle spinning in the air. Dropping the hoe, he ran around the tent covering the grave towards the shed. He searched the workbench for something small and sharp that would fit into the tiny hole on the bottom of the buckle. On the bench he found a tin can filled with rusty finishing nails. He took one and inserted it up into the hole on the buckle. Holding onto the nail, he gave the buckle a flip with his finger. It spun around. He flipped it again and the buckle spun around a dozen times. Flipping it a third time, he watched closely as both sides blended together forming a single, clear image. With continuous flips he was able to see a whole picture that included what looked like the Cooper house, the shed he was standing in, and what seemed to be a rocky outcrop on the side opposite the house. These three items were connected with a wiggly line. Billy spun the buckle again to confirm the image. *The wiggly line must be the tunnel that starts at the cellar of the house and leads to the shed,* he thought. It was a map that someone, at one time, wanted to keep secret. *The bricked-up wall must have been constructed to stop anyone from entering the house through the tunnel.*

Billy walked to the section of floor in the shed that seemed to be hollow and jumped up and down. He listened to the echo. He inspected the floor again. There was no obvious entrance. *Perhaps the person who had built the brick wall had also boarded up the floor of the shed.*

Billy left the shed with the buckle and the finishing nail tucked away in his pocket. He walked over to the cedar tree and looked out to the freeway. It was mid-morning and the traffic was light. Between the two sides of the freeway was a copse of fir trees surrounding a rocky outcrop that reached at least 5-metres higher than the surface of the road. Remembering the image on the spinning belt buckle, he realized it was a map of a tunnel that led from the Cooper place to the rocky outcrop in the middle of the freeway. He figured the tunnel must be very old and probably did not exist anymore for the map was made before the freeway. The road builders had probably destroyed it. Unless...

The freeway was uphill from his present location. *Maybe the tunnel was still there?* Maybe it went right under the freeway and up to the top of the rocky hill on the median between the east and westbound lanes.

Billy felt a rush of goose bumps dance up and down his spine. If he couldn't get into the tunnel from this side, maybe he could find the opening on the median between the freeway lanes. Crossing the freeway during the day was impossible. Traffic was crazy. Someone might be able to cross at night, though—very late at night. He forced his thoughts to settle and walked back to the shed where he had left the hoe and the wheelbarrow.

Just as he approached, he heard a *pssst* from above. He did not look up. He whispered back, "Jackie, is that you?"

"Of course, it's me," replied Jackie. "Is the coast clear? I have to see this tree house, aka secret hideout."

Billy dropped the hoe again. "Let me check," he said, and he walked toward the house. He climbed the back steps and listened. The motor in his father's new screw gun hummed and stopped and then hummed again. He stepped off the porch and ran back to the shed. "My dad is in the house working; if you're quick you can check it out from the ground. No climbing the tree. If he comes out, you gotta hide or you will give away the secret maple tree passage. Once you are on the roof, climb down the pallets on the back wall."

"Okay," said Jackie.

Billy noticed the large branch of the maple tree was bent much closer to the roof of the shed than usual when Jackie made his surprise visits. Jackie hopped off the branch. "I guess this is a good time to tell you that the rest of the gang is here, too. I couldn't keep them away."

Soon the whole gang was standing on the roof of the shed and staring down at Billy.

Billy kept glancing at the house. There was nothing to do but make the best of what appeared to be a very bad situation. "Okay. But if my dad comes out and sees you all, you have to tell him that you all decided to take a walk to see where I was working—or it is goodbye secret passage and goodbye secret hideout. Is everyone clear?"

Jackie opened his mouth to protest.

My way, Jackie!" Billy said.

"Okay, okay," he said and turned to the whole gang standing behind him, "I will do the talking if we get caught. You guys just nod your heads like you agree with whatever I say. Got it?" Everyone nodded their heads in agreement. They all followed Jackie to the edge of the roof and climbed down the leaning pallets.

When everyone was assembled, Billy pointed at the cedar tree. "See that old stump behind the tree?" he asked and waited for them all to acknowledge what he was pointing at. "On my signal you are going to run, one at a time, to that stump, and hide behind it. Look at the cleats on the cedar tree and follow them up until you see the platform. Then peek out at me, quickly wave, and wait for me to signal you to come back. No dawdling. When I do this," he pointed two fingers at them as if they were a pretend gun, "you will run straight back here. Questions?"

"How long can we look?" asked Binky.

Billy rolled his eyes. "You can look to a count of 10."

"Can I count out loud?"

Jackie butted in, "No, Anthony, you have to count in your head. If you cannot count as far as ten then count to five twice." Binky nodded.

"Jackie, you are first." Billy stepped out far enough to see the back porch and then pointed his fingers at Jackie. Jackie ran straight to the stump and disappeared.

Everyone was staring at the stump. Billy looked down at Binky. His mouth was moving as he counted silently to ten. When he got to ten he reached up and pulled on Billy's sleeve and said, "It is past ten. I got to thirteen."

"Don't worry, Binky. He just counts a little slower than you, that's all." This seemed to satisfy him. When Billy looked back at the stump he could see Jackie's hand waving. He glanced over at the house and, seeing the coast was clear, pointed his fingers at Jackie.

Jackie sprinted back to the shed. He was excited, "This is going to be the best secret hideout ever!" His excitement was contagious, and everyone wanted to go next. Billy tapped Sharming on the shoulder and off he sprinted. He chose Binky next. Binky beamed at not being chosen last and dashed off to the stump. They all followed one at a time. The last to go was Orph. She didn't seem to mind. She dashed over to the old stump.

Everyone had stopped counting to ten except Binky. "Orph must be a slow counter because I'm already at twenty," he said.

They all waited and stared at the stump. Suddenly Petra pointed and burst out, "Look. She is up there." Everyone's eyes followed her finger. They could see Orph waving from three meters up the tree.

Orph's head was peeking out from behind the trunk. Suddenly, she ducked back and disappeared. A few seconds later she was running from behind the stump before Billy could signal that all was safe. She dashed up to them with panic in her eyes. She whispered loudly, "The cops. The cops are coming. Someone called the cops. They just drove into the driveway. There is a white van behind them. We have to get out of here."

There was a look of panic in Billy's eyes. "They've come for the body."

Orph's mouth fell open. "There's a body!?"

Billy could hear the car tires on the gravel. He glanced out from behind the shed. His friends had not seen the police tape or the tent that was set up at the front of the shed. "Follow me and don't talk. I will explain later." He quickly led them single file to the shed door and pointed inside. "Go under the bench and cover yourselves with that old green tarp. Hurry. Don't come out until I come and get you. Be quiet."

He had just closed the door and picked up the hoe when his father called from the porch, "William, the police have brought the people from the university. They are going to take the body today."

The police returned to their vehicle. The white van came and parked right beside the tent. Billy stood leaning on his hoe, watching them. They nodded at him and entered the tent. A few minutes later a woman came out and walked over to Billy. "I understand you found this grave. I am really glad you called it in."

"My dad called the police, and I think they called you," said Billy.

"However it happened, I'm glad we have this chance to document some of the history of this place. Old bones often help."

"How long will it take for you guys to dig him up?"

"Oh, we are not going to dig him up today. We are just going to spend a half hour or so figuring out what we need to get the job done. We will be back on Monday."

Billy nodded and watched. His insides were swirling. He prayed his friends could stay quiet for that long. He stood and watched as the university people carried recording equipment into the tent. Camera flashes lit up the canvas. It didn't take as long as they said. Soon they were loading the cameras back into the van and preparing to leave. The woman approached Billy, "We will be here at 8:00 sharp on Monday morning. Please keep an eye on this site while you're here. We don't want anyone messing with our research." She smiled and got back into the van and drove away. Billy started to hoe the garden again to make it look like everything was normal. As soon as the van was out of sight, he dropped the hoe and ran back to the shed.

Billy opened the door of the shed and whispered, "All clear. You guys can come out now."

Sharma was the first out from under the tarp. He was holding his nose. "Thank all of the Indian gods. Petra farted under the tarp. I thought I was going to die."

Petra grinned. "Girls don't fart. We pass pleasant-smelling wind. That's what my mom always says to my dad."

The rest of the gang were all waving their hands in front of their faces. "You're disgusting," said Orph.

"Oh, and you've never farted," said Petra with distain.

"Enough about farts. You guys have to get out of here before my dad hears you and comes to check out the noise. Climb back up onto the roof of the shed and disappear into the maple." He shooed them out the door and around the back of the shed. Once everyone was on the roof he called out in a loud whisper, "Tomorrow at 9, in the tree. I will be last, and I want everyone already here. No latecomers."

Everyone nodded and disappeared into the leaves.

FORT BUILDING AND NEW DISCOVERIES

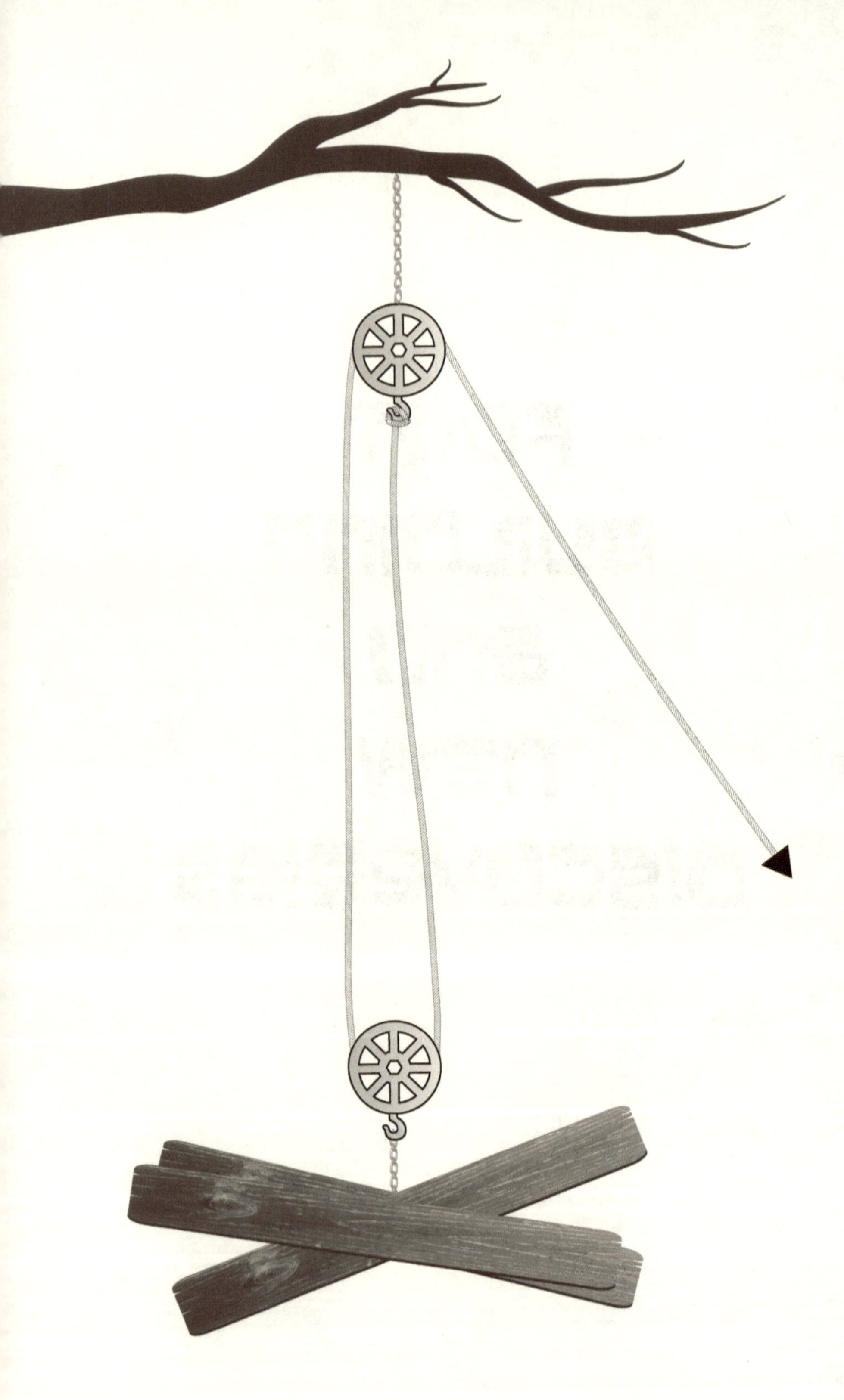

CHAPTER 10

They started on Saturday morning, and by noon they had most of the pallet lumber ready. Everyone had brought a hand tool. They had hammers, crowbars big and small, screwdrivers, and hatchets. All had been borrowed from various workbenches. The Braves sat down and ate their lunch and chatted about sleeping in their new hideout.

Then came the hoist. This was Jackie's masterpiece. He had taken a set of clothes-line pulleys his dad had removed when he got his mom a new dryer. From the two pulleys and some rope he made what he called a *treeler,* short for tree-wheeler. The top pulley was tied to a high tree branch. They could then attach things, like pieces of lumber, to the bottom pulley and pull down on the rope. According to Jackie, his system had a mechanical advantage of two. He explained to everyone how his system cut the weight of the wood hauled up the tree in half, but they would have to pull twice as much rope.

Sharming was about to go into all the other possibilities if they had one more pulley but Orph shut him down with, "Pull—don't talk."

The afternoon was spent lifting the cleats up to Billy, who screwed them to the tree, attaching a large lag eye screw above each cleat for the safety clip on a rope tied to his belt. He had a rule for anyone who climbed the tree. They had to have two ropes about a metre long tied to their belt or around their waist with a safety clip called a carabiner on the end of each rope. They could *not* go up without it. You had to clip onto the lag screw eye, step up on the next cleat, clip on the second eye with the second clip and remove the previous one. Each step would involve the sequence: clip-1 on—step—clip-2 on—clip-1 off—step—clip-1 on—step—clip-2 off, and so on until you reach the platform. If you slipped, there would always be one of the clips attached to the tree. "Safety first," stressed Billy. "If one of us falls and gets hurt our parents will stop us from spending the summer in the best secret hideout ever. I expect all of you to find a way to get yourselves equipped with rope and safety clips." Everyone nodded their head. "Good, now let's clean up. We can never leave stuff out around the yard or my dad will become suspicious. I am going to climb to the platform and move the top pulley into a better position; you guys tie all the leftover lumber to the *treeler* and pull it up. I will lay it out on the platform. Tomorrow we will start on the walls. We have to have walls if we are going to sleep up there."

"And a roof," said Jackie. "I think I can get us a camouflage tarp to use as a roof." Everyone nodded and smiled for the secret hideout promised the best summer ever.

All the Braves were feeling a strong sense of friendship and camaraderie. They all climbed up the last pallet that remained leaning up against the back of the shed and into the maple tree. Billy stayed behind. "I have to do one last check to make sure we did not forget anything. I will see you guys tomorrow at the same time."

The rustling leaves of the maple tree quieted as the gang left the tree, one at a time. Billy scanned the yard for anything that might give them away. It all looked good. The day was warm, and the breeze was light. The roof of the police tent rippled. He turned and looked around. There was no one anywhere in sight. He backed up until his hand touched the tent. He felt the opening slit. He ducked underneath the yellow tape and slipped into the tent. Everything was the same as before, except some of the rotten boards were piled on the side. More of the skeleton was exposed. Billy could see the skull. The bottom of the jaw was at an odd angle to the top jaw. It was missing front teeth.

Billy stared. He didn't think he was scared. He didn't feel scared. It was, after all, just a very old bunch of bones. He knelt on one knee to get a closer look. As soon as his knee settled into the soft earth he saw the bottom jaw bone teeter and fall into the mouth of the skull. Billy startled and jumped back, caught his feet on the pile of casket boards, and fell against the wall of the tent. The entire tent shimmied. He scrambled to his feet. Immediately he recognized what had happened. The university people had balanced the jaw bone, and when he disturbed the ground it simply fell. He looked down and noticed that he had kicked a lot of earth around when he fell. He carefully got down on his knees. He reached for the jaw bone that had settled in the soft earth and quickly withdrew his hand. He kept thinking that a person used to eat food with this jaw. An image of a zombie with its teeth clacking together filled his mind. He shook his head to dispel the image. Quickly grabbing the jaw bone, he rebalanced it on the skull and brushed the dry earth, so it was as smooth as when he had entered. He continued as he backed out, so no one would notice he had ever been inside the tent.

Both the tent and the ancient skeleton would be gone on Monday and he would not miss it. Billy opened the door to the shed. The tarp that the Braves had hidden under was spread across the middle of the floor. He picked it up and rolled it into a tube and tied it with a piece of string left on the workbench. It was not big enough to make a roof for the hideout, but it was good for hiding under if the situation presented itself again. He looked at the wall opposite the bench. There was a line of hooks with all sorts of little items dangling. There were bits of bailing wire, a couple of old ball caps, some leather straps, and bits of hose—long since rotten. Billy walked over and attempted to hang the rolled-up tarp from one of the hooks. The hook held for a few seconds and then gave way. A heavy metal flat bar about a meter long clanged to the floor followed by the tarp. The rolled-up tarp, along with the metal bar, had exceeded the weight the rusty hook could hold. Billy leaned down to pick everything up when he noticed a slot in the floor a couple of centimeters from the wall. It was about two-centimeters wide and fifty long. It ran parallel to the wall. It was nearly invisible from the other side of the room due to the board nailed in front of it.

Billy dropped the tarp. He thought of the hollow sound beneath the shed floor. He looked closer at the flat metal bar. It was pointed at one end. The slot—the flat metal bar— the hollow floor. Like puzzle pieces, they all came together in his mind, and Billy fitted the bar into the slot. The hole beneath must have been designed to allow the bar to slip perfectly into whatever was down below. Billy looked at the bar protruding from the floor at an angle, the flat side toward the wall. He did to the bar what it looked like the configuration was designed to do. He grabbed onto it and pulled like you would a lever. It moved very slowly. Billy pulled harder until the bar was just past upright, then he did not need to pull anymore. The bar travelled the rest of the way on its own. There was a rumbling, then a twang, as if something heavy had pulled something taut. There was a moment of silence, a creak of boards, a scream of metal, and finally a bang. A section of the floor opened behind him. It was supported by a set of rusty spring hinges attached from below. They had been compressed for a long time. Billy felt that they had screamed with joy to be finally set free.

The section of the floor that opened was not a perfect rectangle. The edges were just the boards sticking out in the pattern that the builder had placed them. This left no indication of a trapdoor in the floor because it looked like a normal floor. Now it was gaping open in the dust-filled room.

Billy crept to the edge and peeked down. He could barely make out the bottom. He could see portions of what appeared to be an old ladder. There was no way down, and if you happened to fall down the hole, there would be no way up. He needed a proper ladder. His dad had ladders, but they were always in use. He would have to build one. That was not a big job if you had the right materials.

His mind raced. He had a million questions that could only be answered if he could get down there and explore. Billy felt a shiver run up and down his spine. The secrets of the old Cooper place were revealing themselves a little at a time. This crazy tunnel, he was now sure, was the secret way into the cellar of the house. Why had it been bricked up? The belt buckle suggested it also went somewhere else—somewhere in the middle of the freeway median. Maybe it even went further. There were a lot of questions that Billy had no answers to. He thought about sharing his discoveries with the gang. His face scrunched up. He did not want to share anything, at least until he had the answers to a few of the questions. This was his discovery. It was his to do with what he pleased. He would tell no one. It would remain his secret for as long as he could keep it.

Billy, ever the practical one, grabbed a piece of string off the work bench, tied an old bolt to one end, and dangled it down the hole in the floor until it touched the ground. He tied a knot in the string at floor level and pulled it up. The hole was a little over seven-feet down. He would have to build his ladder longer so that it would sit at an angle. An eight-foot ladder would barely fit in the shed and would be very obvious. Billy started designing one in his head that would fold in half. It could fit discreetly under the workbench when not in use. He would unfold it, open the trapdoor, drop the ladder down, explore, climb back up the ladder, put it away, and finally, close the trapdoor.

Close the trapdoor? He suddenly realized he did not know how to close the door in the floor. His secret would be very short lived if he could not close it. He pushed on the upright trapdoor. Old springs creaked and squeaked on either side of the door at its base. He pushed, and the door slowly began to close. As it got closer to the floor and the springs became more compressed it became harder and harder to close. Finally, Billy was standing on the closed trapdoor. He started to step off and realized that whatever held the door in place was not working. The door was primed to spring open the moment his weight came off. He jumped up and down in the hope that he might jar whatever needed jarring and the lock would click into place. He looked at the lever still protruding from the floor. Maybe he had to pull the lever back in place before he tried to shut it. He walked toward the hinges of the trapdoor and turned. He did not want it to bang like the time before. He slowly eased it up until he could grab the edge and caught it in his hands. It was now fully open again.

Billy walked over to the lever and pushed it back to its original position. It required all of his strength. There were creaking and banging sounds before it finally reached the starting position. He gingerly took his hand away, and the lever stayed in place. He started to close the trapdoor again, but this time he heard a resounding click as it finally settled. The floor was a floor again. There was nothing to indicate that there was ever a trapdoor there, except the boards that were part of the trapdoor were now cleaner than the rest of the floor. The dirt had fallen off when it was upright. Billy quickly brushed the dirt around until it was evenly distributed again. Then he picked up the tarp, tossed it on the bench, and left the shed. This tunnel would remain secret, known to him and only him until he learned more of the ancient secrets it was hiding.

a BUILDING PARTY and DARK TUNNELS

CHAPTER 11

The plan for Sunday was to meet in the maple tree at 9:00 a.m. Everyone was to try and make a safety belt with two ropes with carabiner clips at the end. If they could, and Billy said it was safe, then they might be able to visit the tree house. There would be no borrowing. Everyone had to have their own safety equipment. Only Maddox had been successful in equipping himself. The rest would have the following week to get the required belt, rope, and clips.

Once on the ground, they all gathered around Maddox and looked at his safety belt. "I had like ten of these clips that I collected last year. They came free on a giant bottle of Gatorade," said Maddox.

Petra slithered up to him. "Hey, dog, how about giving me a couple of those?"

"Whacha got to trade? These are pretty cool, and they

might come in handy later."

Petra pinched her chin with her crooked finger and thumb. "I will grant you a favor the next time you ask for something."

Maddox cocked his head to the side. "Doubt there is anything I would need from you, but I will tell you what." He looked up at everyone. "I have enough of these for everyone but only as a loaner. I want them back when the summer is over."

They all nodded their heads and promised to return any clips he loaned them. "We have our Monday meeting on the lawn. I will bring them."

Maddox and Billy climbed up to the tree house and fixed the pulley system, so that they could pull up the lumber and build a railing around the edge of the platform. It was about three meters wide and four meters long. The tree came up near the edge of the platform near the middle. The main platform stuck out on the freeway side, making it difficult to see if you did not know it was there. Jackie and the rest of the gang attached the materials to the bottom pulley and then they all hauled on the rope, lifting the materials to the platform where Billy and Maddox untied them and sent the pulley down for the next load. It took five lifts to get everything they had collected onto the platform.

Billy came down the tree and called a meeting to order. "We have not collected enough materials to build proper walls and a roof. If we are going to use it safely, we have to do this right. All the lumber up there is going to have to be used to fix the floor. After I inspected it, I noticed a few spots that are weak. I suggest that Maddox and I fix the floor, and you guys spend the rest of the day scavenging. We need more lumber—like two by fours and some plywood. Even small pieces will work. We can use it for the roof. Screws and nails, too. Oh, and a good tarp. Once we have a solid roof, we can use the tarp to keep the rain out."

The afternoon zipped by. Maddox and Billy fitted the pallet boards in a neat pattern over the entire floor of old lookout platform while the rest of the gang returned to the Glen to look for materials. Billy had not borrowed a saw, so the boards just stuck out in a random pattern over the edges. He would cut them off when they were done. The end result was, in Billy's mind, almost perfect. The boards varied in thickness, but they were all the same width. Both he and Maddox sat with their backs to the tree trunk where it passed through the platform. They scanned their efforts. "Looks good, Billy Boy," said Maddox.

"Yeah, sure does."

"Yep. Perfect," he said and gazed out at the view. "You can sure see a long way from up here."

"Yeah. It's going to be cool to spend the night here," said Billy.

"When do you think we will be finished?"

"That all depends on when we find the wood to finish it. We can work on weekends and after six in the evening. It will only take three or four days if everyone does their share."

Maddox's ears perked; he could hear someone calling from over the wall, inside the Glen. Someone was calling him. "That's my sister. I gotta go." He climbed down the tree moving from cleat to cleat, taking the time to clip and unclip from the screw eyes. He was quick and soon reached the bottom. He looked back up at Billy and called, "Hey, Billy, I am going to leave my safety belt in the shed." Billy gave him a thumbs up. He watched as Maddox entered the shed, returned and climbed onto the roof, then disappeared into the leaves of the maple tree.

Billy leaned back and smiled. He had pretty much organized this whole secret hideout thing. He felt good. He was a good leader. He was looking after his gang like he was supposed to. He stared at the outcrop in the middle of the freeway median. It was surrounded by young fir trees with a couple of alder thrown in. The brush was dense where the trees ended. Some of it had new blackberry bushes climbing down the slope to the edge of the roadway. He could not see an easy path to the rock tower. Down the median, the trees gradually decreased in size. *Some could be perfect Christmas trees,* he thought, taking note to remember that for next year. He could sneak across when the traffic was light and chop one down. Dragging it back across the busy road was another matter. A guy could get killed crossing that road. The speed limit was over 120 kph, but almost everyone went faster.

He glanced back at the maple tree. He was alone and there was at least two hours before he was due home. Climbing down the cedar tree, he found himself not always following his own rules. He felt comfortable with the system of cleats and stopped clipping-on halfway down. He decided he would only do this when he was alone. Once down, he entered the shed and removed the safety belt. He felt an urge to explore the newly discovered trapdoor in the shed floor, but there was no point if he couldn't climb down into the pit below. Wondering if his father may have left one of his ladders in the Cooper house, he walked to the back door and up onto the porch. Laying on the floor of the porch was a six-foot step ladder. He grabbed it and rushed back to the shed. His plan was to tie a piece of rope to the ladder, tie the other end to the bench, open the ladder, and lower the open ladder down into the hole. He figured he should be able to lower himself onto the top step of the ladder and climb down into the hole. Getting out would be easy, and all he would need to do was pull the ladder back up by the rope and return it to the porch.

Billy inserted the metal bar into the slot—the way he had the day before—and pulled. The trapdoor swung open with a creak and a bang. Billy made a mental note to oil the springs and ease the door up more slowly. He prepared the ladder and was soon stepping off the bottom rung. He had brought a small flashlight with him and turned it on. He was standing in a cavern with tunnels leading off in two directions: one toward the house and one toward the road. Each tunnel narrowed and fled into spider web filled darkness. Billy felt a chill that was partly due to the cool earth surrounding him and partly due to a sort of fearful excitement. He decided to explore the tunnel that lead back to the house. Billy could walk down the tunnel completely upright, though a grown man would have to crouch down. The ceiling was so close that Billy had to duck the occasional root that had grown through the earth above. Every so often, there were wooden supports to stop possible cave-ins. After a short while, Billy stopped. A brick wall was blocking the path. It must be the other side of the wall he found behind the cupboard in the Cooper house cellar. There were still a few unused bricks piled at the base of the wall. He picked one up and tapped the wall in various places. It was solid and impassable.

Billy turned back and returned to the ladder below the shed. The other end of the tunnel led towards the freeway. He stared into the darkness. A shiver coursed its way up and down his spine and out his fingertips. He felt a little like Indiana Jones, except he had a flashlight and not a giant flaming torch. He pointed the light into the tunnel. The beam was bright but narrow—a mini spotlight that pierced the blackness, like a laser-thin beam of light that splashed out where it hit the moisture seeping from the walls. He took three more steps forward. The floor began to slope down, and the first of many supports came into view. They were still solid and smelled faintly of the creosote used to stop rot. A smell he recognized because of a job he'd helped his father with last summer. The further he went down the tunnel the more apprehensive he became. He turned and pointed his flashlight back the way he had come. The light hit the wall behind him, and he realized the tunnel was not only sloping down but curving to the left. The walls were no longer dirt. They were now solid rock. He shivered, but this time it was with the cold. He pointed his light at the wall. It was a natural tunnel that the builders had tapped into. The walls were damp, and there were no more supports. He was not sure how far he had walked, but the flashlight was definitely dimmer. The batteries were going dead. He stopped. The thought of crawling back through a cold, wet, dark tunnel was enough to make him turn around and head back. He was rushing this time and shortly he saw a glow and then the ladder standing like a sentry in a pool of yellow light coming from the shed above. It looked eerily alive, as if it were waiting to take Billy and lead him to safety. He climbed the ladder, pulled it out of the cavern with the rope, closed the trapdoor, and returned the ladder to the porch. As he left the porch he began to consider how he might put lights down into the cave below the shed. It would be more like the home base of the tunnel. It would also make the tunnel less threatening. Billy was not afraid of darkness. He had been in the dark many times. It was what might come out of the darkness that frightened him.

THE
EXCAVATION

The next morning, Billy was at work again. His father had dropped him off and gone to do a plumbing job on the other side of the Glen. Billy was hoeing and wheeling the roots to the pile. He was on his third wheelbarrow when a white van with university markings on the side drove up the driveway, over the back grass that was mostly dandelions, and right up to the tent surrounded by the yellow police tape. Two men, and the woman he had previously spoken to, got out of the van. The woman approached him while the men removed a stretcher from the back of the van. They set it to the side and began to take down the yellow tape. They rolled up the sunward side of the tent and light streamed in.

Billy leaned on his hoe and smiled at the woman. "Come to get the skeleton?"

"Yes. We will place it, bone by bone, on the stretcher,

cover it and transport it to our lab. You can watch if you won't get too creeped out." She grinned and turned to assist the men. Soon they were all on their knees at the grave with the stretcher on one side. Billy stood at one end and watched them.

They pulled one bone at a time out of the grave and placed it on the stretcher in its normal location. The man in the middle picked up the pelvis and a number of other bones came with it, held in place by what looked like a leather strap. They fell back into the hole as the strap disintegrated. "Looks like he was wearing a belt. There must be a buckle here somewhere. I doubt whoever buried him would remove it," said the man as his gloved hand felt around in the dirt in search of it. Billy felt his face turn red. He quickly stepped back, so they could not see his reaction. The buckle felt warm in his pocket. "Nothing here."

"Too bad. That might have given us a clue about who he was. Hey, look at this," the man said and pulled out a half-disintegrated old boot with a bony foot still inside.

"The boot might give us a clue about when this happened. We might be able to date it from the type of material used in the sole, which is pretty much intact," said the other man.

Billy backed up further. He felt less guilty for not mentioning the buckle. He figured the boot would help them more than an old brass buckle.

The woman stood at the head of the grave, and Billy shivered when she lifted the skull out of the dry earth and dusted it off with a paint brush. She turned it to look at the teeth. She spoke to her companions, "The front teeth are missing, but the remainder looks to be in good shape. There are no cavities, which suggests he lost his front teeth by accident. Perhaps he was in a fight. He does not appear to be very old. These teeth suggest he was between 25 and 40." She held up the skull and looked at it face on.

The man beside her pointed at the front of the skull. "I am pretty sure this is how he died."

The woman examined a jagged hole in the bone. "This is not good. It looks like he was hit in the head with something sharp or..."

Billy could not hear what they said next because they whispered to each other. The woman and the man at the opposite end unfurled the tent flap, concealing the three archeologists. He took a step closer to the tent, but all he could make out was a murmur of voices. One of the men stepped out of the tent and walked to the van. He went to the back, removed a series of mesh screens set in wood frames and carried them to the tent. He did not speak or look in Billy's direction.

Billy moved closer and pretended to be digging out roots. He could just barely hear the three inside the tent.

"It must have fallen out when you picked it up."

"Check there first."

There were digging sounds, scraping, and the rattle of small stones on the screens as they filtered the earth from the grave.

"There," the woman said.

"Nope. Just a rock."

There were more screening sounds and then the woman spoke again, "Look! I found it. It is a bit misshapen, but it is defin—" The sound of two shovels clanking together as they dropped to the ground blocked out the rest of the sentence. The three inside the tent stopped speaking. They continued to sift the soil in the grave. Finally, they came out of the tent and rolled up the side. They lifted the stretcher out of the tent and placed it in the back of the van along with all their tools. They removed the tent and set it to the side. The woman turned toward Billy. "We won't be much longer. We will take the casket boards and try to date them. I will leave the tent here for the police to pick up. I have to call them anyway. Do you want us to fill in the hole?"

Billy looked around. "Nah—I have a bunch of rocks I have to bury. I can just toss them in there and shove some dirt around. Thanks anyway." He gestured to the skeleton. "Will we be able to find out who he was—that's if you figure it out?"

"Sure," said the woman. She reached under the apron she was wearing, pulled out a business card, and handed it to him. "My number is on there. Give us a call in a couple of months and maybe I will be able to tell you."

Billy took the card and nodded. A few minutes later the three were finished. They collected their tools and waved goodbye as they drove away.

Billy continued to lean on his hoe. He stared down at the hole in the ground. All remnants of the skeleton and the casket were gone. On an urge, Billy walked over to the grave, knelt down, and ran his hands through the dry soil. He was not sure why, but he felt that they might have missed something. After a few passes, he decided there was nothing there. He stood up and took out the buckle and spun it on the nail. It was definitely a map of the tunnel. It stopped spinning, and he looked at it more carefully. The outer edge of the buckle looked like it had some sort of markings he had not noticed before. They were very faded, as if constant rubbing had worn them away. Billy took his thumbnail and scratched at the edge. He peered again and thought maybe he could see the markings more clearly. He spit and scraped some more, but he could not make them any clearer. He flipped the buckle to the other edge and scraped it too. There was something etched into the brass for sure. He peered at the markings but could not make them out. He decided to check them out with a magnifying glass when he got to the privacy of his room and slipped the buckle back into his pocket.

Billy picked up a boulder and dropped it into the grave hole. He was about to pick up another when he heard his dad drive into the Cooper driveway. His dad got out of the truck and walked toward him. "They got it moved already. I didn't expect them until this afternoon," said his dad while staring down into the grave. "Good. Fill it up with rocks. I am supposed to create a brick pathway to the shed and it will go right over this."

"The university people said that they would call the police to pick up their tent," said Billy.

"Good. Want to go for lunch? I fancy some sushi. What do you think?" His father grinned. Billy loved sushi, especially dynamite rolls. He dropped his hoe and walked with his father to the truck.

SLEEP
OUT
PLANS

July was half over. The weather was hot and humid. Billy got to leave the Cooper place early. The Gang had worked hard on the hideout all week and it was almost at a point where they could sleepover. Billy had given everyone a day off. The gang was looking forward to a night in their new fort. Billy was still concerned that it might not be safe. He was pragmatic and considered all possible ways that sleeping in the fort might prove dangerous. Sitting in Jackie's room on his bean-bag chair, Billy listened to Jackie.

"How about this weekend? It's completed to a point where we could all sleep there overnight. Let's tell the guys."

"I want you to imagine something."

"What?" asked Jackie, slightly exasperated.

"Imagine we are all up in the fort. Everyone is asleep,

and Binky wakes up 'cause he has to pee."

"I already thought of that. I made a hole in the wall for our *you know what's*. He can stick it out and pee." Jackie crossed his arms and looked at Billy, seeming confident that he had countered his argument.

"What about Petra and Orph? They are not going to be happy with your plan. They will have to climb down, pee in the bushes, and climb back up. All that in the pitch dark. That is not safe."

"I know! My grandma was sick last year at our house and she used a potty thing. Bed pan—that's what it's called! They can pee in that and empty it in the morning."

"Can you get it?"

"Of course. It is sitting in the bathroom cupboard under the sink. No one will miss it."

"Good. Maybe we can even make a small bathroom area near the hole and hang up a sheet or something. Petra would want privacy. For that matter, so would Sharming."

"It's decided then. Once we are settled in for the night, no one goes down until morning. That way no one will kill themselves in the middle of the night."

"I still think it needs to be tested out. What about just you and me sleeping up there one night just to make sure?"

"Good idea, Billy Boy! How about tonight?"

Billy paused. He knew if they were to keep the hideout a secret they would have to lie to their parents. Billy didn't like to lie, but sometimes it was necessary. The bad thing about lying was the guilt and, of course, getting caught. He wondered about his dad's reaction if he lied and was found out. The images that followed were not pleasant, to say the least. If he said he was sleeping at Jackie's house and his dad phoned and he wasn't there then ... not good.

"Billy? What about it? I'll tell my parents I'm at your house and you the same."

Billy considered. What if he were to tell his dad the truth, just not the whole truth. If something went wrong at least he could say that he did not lie. "I can't lie to my dad."

"What do you mean? If you tell him, he will bring all our parents into it and all that work will be for nothing."

"I said I cannot lie about this. It's too risky. You do whatever you feel will work."

"What are you going to tell him?"

"I am going to tell him that we built a secret fort and we are going to have a sleepover in the secret fort." Billy paused. "When he asks me where the fort is I am going to tell him that it is a secret. I am going to explain that I have made sure that it is safe. I think he will allow me to spend the night. He will think that it is in the Glen and he knows that he could find any fort we might make in the Glen if he had to. I will leave out the part about it being thirty-feet in the air at the edge the Cooper place overlooking the freeway. If I tell him that then he might say "No" and tell me it's just too dangerous."

"Billy, that is just brilliant. We'll tell everyone to do that. If their parents say they still can't come that is their problem. They cannot, under any circumstances, tell anyone outside the gang where the fort is located." He thought for a moment. "Everyone except Binky. He is too young, and I know he will mess up. I recommend that we just don't tell him when we are going to sleep over."

"That is a pretty nasty thing to do to him, but I agree. He will just have to wait until next year when he is older."

"So. Tonight?" Jackie fluttered his eyebrows up and down and smiled. "What do you say, Oh Bodacious One?"

Billy jumped off the bean-bag chair and tackled Jackie. He started to give him a noogie.

Jackie squealed and pushed him away.

Billy stood. "Pack a sleeping bag, a foamy, and a flashlight. See if you can get some food. I will do the same. I will meet you out in front of your house at 8:30."

Billy left Jackie's house and headed home. His dad had

said that he would be late and to make dinner ready at 6:00. Billy got home at 4:30. He opened the fridge and saw the main ingredient intended for dinner. Billy was a good cook. In fact, he loved to cook. He had two meals he was good at making: chicken breasts smeared with mayo covered with bread crumbs and powdered parmesan cheese baked in the oven; and meat loaf. Tonight, was meatloaf night because the meat was sitting front and center in the fridge. He took out the package of ground beef, ground pork, and ground veal. Billy searched for the other ingredients and placed them on the counter. He looked at what he had: the meat, one egg, some bread crumbs, some BBQ sauce (extra spicy), salt and pepper, and two slices of bacon. He knew his father would put onions in it, but Billy thought they were disgusting, so he left them out. After all, he was the cook, and the cook got to make it the way he wanted.

He washed his hands, and then dumped everything into a large bowl, except the BBQ sauce and the bacon. He stuck his hands into the bowl and mixed it up, letting the mixture ooze between his fingers. When it was fully mixed, he patted it down in a loaf-pan, squeezed the BBQ sauce on the top, and covered that with the bacon. He turned the oven up to 350-degrees, set the timer for an hour and fifteen minutes, and cleaned up. He tossed a couple of potatoes in the oven and sliced a tomato to serve as the vegetable. Et voila—he was done.

His father appeared to be in a good mood. He said he'd put a bid in on a new job, and it had been accepted. Billy thought this would be the best time to ask him about the sleep out. His dad didn't seem to mind, but he did ask the question that Billy knew he would.

"Where is this clubhouse?"

"Secret clubhouse," replied Billy.

"So where is this secret club house?" Billy looked at him and shrugged. "Oh, I see. It is a secret, so you are not going to tell me."

"A secret must be kept, otherwise..."

"Otherwise it loses its appeal. I get it. I had a number of secret clubhouses when I was a kid. The thing is they didn't stay secret for long. But it was cool while they were. Okay. You can keep your secret, but please be safe."

"I have taken care to keep everyone safe. The gang depends on me."

"They do, eh? Well, William, I think that is a good thing. Have fun."

"Jackie and I were going to try it out tonight to make sure everything is okay before the whole gang sleeps over. We're going to invite everyone for Saturday night. That okay?"

"No problem," said his dad as he picked up the remote and started to watch the news. He looked up at Billy. "Oh, yeah—great meatloaf." He grinned and continued, "even if there were no onions."

Billy went to his room and started to pack his things.

THE WITNESSES

CHAPTER 14

Billy stood with his back to a tree on the boulevard in front of Jackie's house. The shadows were long, the sun about to catch the edge of the fence. After disappearing behind it, the trip to the maple tree would be easy, for the shadows would conceal their actions. As usual, Jackie was late. Billy sighed and slid to a sitting position with his back to the tree. He set his backpack between his legs and closed his eyes. A moment later his mind took him to the tunnel. He was imagining what was beyond the section where he had stopped. Next time he would take a geek light that fit on his forehead and a backup flashlight. He needed to find a time to go all the way to the end. The brass buckle seemed to suggest that the tunnel ended at the rocky outcrop on the median between the two sides of the freeway. He wondered what he might find there. Sometime in the past, this tunnel led directly to the forge in the cellar of the Cooper house. A forge was used for melting metal. Why would someone want to keep that a secret? When he was cleaning up, he saw a number of brass figurines in the cellar. The secret part still bothered him. His mind was wandering again when he heard a faint snapping noise. He opened his eyes just before Jackie jumped on him and whispered, "Boo."

Jackie fell over on the ground laughing. "I scared you."

Billy climbed to his feet. "You did not." He grabbed his pack and foamy, looked cautiously around, and started walking to the old maple. "Come on. It's getting dark. I want a bit of sunlight to setup on the platform."

Soon they'd dropped to the shed roof at the back of the Cooper property. They climbed down to the ground, looked around, and made their way to the base of the giant cedar. "I will go up first and drop the rope. You tie the stuff on to the rope. I will haul it up while you climb up," said Billy.

"Sounds like a plan," said Jackie. He dropped his bag and foamy on top of Billy's.

A few minutes later, they were both laying on their sleeping bags, staring up the tree while the sun slowly disappeared behind a copse of fir trees on the other side of the freeway.

"What did you bring for snacks?" asked Jackie.

"You were supposed to bring the food."

"I did, but I just assumed you would bring something in case I forgot. What did you bring, Billy Boy?"

Billy sat up and grabbed his backpack. He reached inside and pulled out some fruit bars. He tossed them to Jackie. He followed the arc of the fruit bars and in the background, he saw a police car with its lights flashing behind a large truck towing a semi-trailer. "Look," he said and pointed down at the freeway. Darkness had settled and the flashing lights, blue and red, splattered the trees on the median. The semi pulled over on the median side of the south-bound freeway lanes. There was no room on the curb side. The police car stopped behind the trailer and two men got out. Billy stared at the car that did not look like a police car. The flashing lights were inside the car and tucked into the car's grill. Billy found it odd that this police car had no lights flashing at the back of the car to warn oncoming drivers that there was an obstruction ahead. He had seen enough cop shows to know.

"Cool," said Jackie.

"I wonder why they pulled that truck over?"

"Probably something wrong with the lights. See, one of those men is checking the lights at the back of the truck.

Where did the other guy go?"

"He walked behind the truck. Probably to talk to the driver." Both Billy and Jackie watched and waited for the second policeman to reappear. "They must be undercover cops."

"Yeah. No uniforms."

The boys continued to watch the events unfolding below. The police man behind the truck picked up a rock from the side of the road. He was framed with light from a passing car. He carried the rock back to the truck and looked around. He even looked at the tree where Jackie and Billy were sitting. He did not dwell on them. The boys were sure they were invisible behind the branches. They could see out, but the men on the road below could not see them. The man seemed satisfied that no one was watching him. The two boys watched him, framed in flashing red and blue light, take the rock and smash one of the tail lights on the truck and toss the rock into the bushes on the median.

"Whoa. Did you just see what that cop did! He smashed the light," said Jackie.

"Holy crap."

"Billy, he smashed the light on purpose," shouted Jackie. Below, the light-smashing policeman looked up. He scanned for witnesses, as if he had heard Jackie shout.

"Shut up. He might hear you," whispered Billy as he pulled down on Jackie's arm to hide him from the cop below. The policeman had not heard him. He stepped to the side, so he could see up the side of the truck that was hidden from Billy and Jackie's view. He pointed at the smashed light. Just then the driver of the truck came into view followed by the other policeman. The driver stared at the broken light. He reached out to touch it and looked down. On the ground he saw pieces of red plastic and bent down to pick one up. He straightened and looked at a shard of red plastic in his hand, looked back at the broken light and looked back at the cops. He pointed at them and became very animated. The boys could see that he was shouting at the policemen. They guessed he had realized that they had just smashed his light. At that point, everything became more animated and happened very quickly. The light-smashing policeman pulled out a gun and pointed it at the driver. The other policeman quickly put handcuffs on the driver. They marched him to the car and opened the car door. The driver tried to backup and turn around. The policeman hit the driver in the head with the butt of his gun and shoved him into the back seat.

"Double crap," whispered Billy. The boys had crouched down and were peering through the cracks and knotholes in the three-foot fence that surrounded the platform. They had built it so no one would fall off in their sleep. Now they were using it to ensure that the men below did not notice that they were witnesses to the events happening on the side of the freeway.

"Maybe that driver is a wanted criminal," said Jackie.

"Why would they smash his light?"

"What are they going to do now?"

As if to answer his question one of the men disappeared down the side of the truck and the other got into the police car and shut off the flashing lights. The truck started to move down the freeway followed by the police car. They soon disappeared from sight.

"I don't get it," said Jackie, now sitting up with his back to the fence. "They should have called for someone to take the truck away. If that guy was arrested, then they would both take him in. They would never have driven the truck. Those big semis require an air-brake license. It is unlikely that a typical cop would even know how to drive one. I know. My uncle drives one and he goes on about how difficult it is to drive one of those big rigs unless, like him, you have had the right training."

Billy shook his head. "I don't know. It was pretty weird." He climbed into his sleeping bag and rolled on to his stomach. "I have to work tomorrow. That means I have to get up early, go home, eat breakfast, and then come back here. I better get some sleep."

"Sleep tight," replied Jackie.

Billy heard him getting his bed ready and then the sound of water falling from a great height.

"Ummm," Jackie began, "I think we're gonna need to find a better place to pee from. I'm pretty sure the wind just blew the pee stream right onto one of the lower climbing rungs."

"Nice, Jackie, nice. You are going down first in the morning to clean it off."

"I said, *I think*. Anyway, it will be dry by morning. You won't even notice. 'Night, Billy Boy."

Billy listened to Jackie get settled in his sleeping bag. He closed his eyes, but sleep did not come. He stared up the tree trunk. The branches swayed in the light breeze. Thoughts of the truck and the police actions he had just witnessed marched through his mind, step by step. After each he stopped and reflected on what had happened. In the end, he was no closer to understanding the why of what he had witnessed. He started over again. He started sooner than before. He started when he first saw the police car lights coming down the highway. It pulled up behind the semi. He inspected the car in his mind. It was an older model sedan. It was not something the police would still be using.

That thought triggered a series of thoughts that resulted in the following realization:

They were not cops, and they stole the truck. Hijacked was a better word. They *hijacked* the truck. Billy sat up. He wanted to wake up Jackie and tell him, but he could hear him breathing rhythmically and decided not to. He lay back down and watched the film in his head one more time. The semi had the name of a large electronics store chain on the side. It was probably filled with top of the line merchandise. The kind of stuff that hijackers could easily sell. What would they do with the driver? Thoughts of murder filled Billy's mind. The driver could be dead right now. They might have killed him to keep him from identifying them. All the ways they might have killed him swirled around in Billy's mind. He forced himself from thinking of it and turned over. Sleep did not come quickly.

TREASURE HUNTING SCHOOL

The next morning, Billy woke at sunrise. Jackie was already awake and sitting cross-legged with his sleeping bag over his shoulders. He was staring down at the freeway pullout. The silence was broken by a car driving toward the city. Jackie turned to Billy. "I don't think they were cops. They stole that truck," he said flatly and turned to Billy. "We gonna tell anyone?"

"Dunno." Billy shrugged.

Jackie nodded, as if he understood that the case was temporarily closed. It was like the light of day had erased the fear they had felt the night before. They packed up and climbed down. Billy jumped off the third step to avoid the possibility of touching a peed-on cleat.

"You're crazy," Jackie said. He pointed at the bottom two cleats. "I must have missed. There's no pee on these."

Billy gave him a thumbs-up, but he was not taking

any chances. They headed for the garden shed, climbed onto the roof and into the maple tree with fruit bars hanging out of their mouths. They parted ways after agreeing to talk to the gang later that day.

Billy dumped his stuff in his room and poured himself some cereal. He sniffed the milk to make sure it was not sour and poured it into the bowl. He ate and waited for his dad to get up. A few minutes later his dad came into the kitchen dressed in his robe. He did not say anything to Billy just walked to the coffee machine and made a morning coffee. He sat down opposite Billy and took a sip.

"How was the sleepover?" his dad asked with little enthusiasm.

"It was okay."

"No problems?"

"No. The whole gang might try it out tonight. That's if their parents let them."

"Sounds like it might be fun. Don't stay up too late."

"Why?"

"Well, I told the university people that I would drop by on Monday and get the lowdown on that skeleton you found at the Cooper's. I thought you might like to come. After all, you discovered it. I'm also dropping off the tent at the police station. Knowing how busy they are, that tent might lay there all summer before they get around to picking it up."

Thoughts of the police both excited and frightened Billy. Knowing whose skeleton it was might also explain the buckle. Maybe they even knew about the tunnel. Billy had kept it a secret. He realized he was keeping a lot of secrets. The buckle, the tunnel, the secret cupboard in the cellar, and now the events on the freeway were all piling up in his head. Only Jackie knew about the freeway. Billy knew he would not tell anyone.

"Are we working today?"

"You will be glad to hear that I am giving you a half day off. We will work this morning and then I have to go into the city. That okay with you?" he asked with a grin.

Billy just grinned back and started to eat his cereal. "I am just about finished digging up the garden bed. What do you want me to do next?"

His dad rubbed his chin whiskers. "The bottom section of siding on the house needs to be painted. It will require some scraping first. The old paint is flaking off. I think I have a wire brush you can used to clean it up before you paint. I will get the paint when I go into the city this afternoon."

"Okay. Those roots are starting to invade my dreams. I

don't think I can do that job much longer without losing my mind."

"I know what you mean. Long tedious jobs tend to wear on a body. That is why I like my job. I get to do a whole lot of different things. You should consider that when you choose your path in life. Any thoughts on what you want to be when you grow up?"

Billy looked up at the ceiling. "Well, lately I have been thinking about becoming a detective or a treasure hunter or both." His father burst into laughter. Billy's face started to turn red. "What's wrong with that?" he retorted. "They are both pretty cool things to do."

"Nothing is wrong; it's just that becoming either of those things requires something else first."

"Like what?"

"Well, a detective usually requires that you become a police officer or criminalist first. A treasure hunter usually means you started out as an archeologist or historian first. Those things require time and study. There are no detective or treasure hunter schools that I know of." He reached out and patted Billy's hand. "William, I didn't mean to burst your bubble." He reconsidered. "On the other hand, a kid with your smarts could probably do anything you want. When we go to the university you can ask about being a treasure hunter. It does sound like an interesting job." He smiled. "Any of that cereal left?"

"Yeah," said Billy. He handed the box to his dad.

A few minutes later, they were on their way to the Cooper place. Billy completed the garden by 10 and started scraping the flaking paint. He worked till noon and was dropped off back home. His dad continued to the city, leaving Billy free for the afternoon.

Billy called Jackie and they decided to call the gang together. That was done by a phone tree. Jackie phoned Petra and Petra phoned someone else and so on until everyone was called. Billy headed out the door with an apple in his pocket and a quickly constructed ham sandwich in his mouth. He sat leaning against the concrete fence on the far side of the boulevard. He was munching on the apple as the gang started to arrive. Petra was first. She plunked down beside him. "I can't wait until we all get our own cell phones. We can just text each other," she said.

"Yeah, right. My dad won't get me a cell phone until I am 15. My sister got hers last year. She is sixteen now."

"Well, I am getting mine on my birthday, but that's not until November. I can't wait."

"Lucky you," said Billy, just as Jackie, Maddox, Orph

and Sharming arrived. Jackie had a backpack slung over his shoulder.

"Who is lucky?" asked Orph overhearing Billy's comment.

Billy ignored the question, not wanting to start a discussion on the possibility of getting a cell phone. "Where's Binky?" He turned to Orph. "Did you call him?" he asked realizing he had forgotten to remind Jackie to exclude him from the phone tree.

"Yeah, but he couldn't come. I talked to his mother, and she said they were going away for the weekend."

"Just as well. I don't think it's a good idea for him to spend the night in the tree house. He is too young."

"How did it go last night? Any problems we need to address before tonight?" asked Petra.

Billy glanced at Jackie. They silently agreed that they would not mention what they now both thought was a hijacking. "Great," said Billy.

"Yeah, great. You can sure see a long ways from up there. I woke up in the middle of the night and the trees were swaying back and forth. It was a little spooky but cool at the same time," said Jackie.

"There is one new rule that I have decided as president of this club," stated Billy.

Jackie butted in, "What rule?"

"I decided that the boys, like the girls, have to pee in a container. No one can pee over the edge. The wind can blow pee all over the climbing cleats. Besides that, it will really stink if everyone pees over the edge. So, the rule is: you hold it, or you bring your own container with a lid."

"It sounds like this pee problem came up last night. Who peed over the edge and where did that pee land?" asked Petra who was now standing with her hands on her hips. She looked from Jackie to Billy and back to Jackie. "Tinker it was you, wasn't it? I bet you peed all over the climbing cleats. God, I hope you cleaned off the cleats."

"I never got any pee on the cleats," replied Jackie defensively.

"Alright," shouted Billy. "Enough pee talk. Does everyone have their harness ready?" Everyone nodded. "Is there anything else?"

"We are going to need food and entertainment," said Orph. "Everyone has to bring something. I can bring cards and a huge bag of peanuts."

"I'll bring chips," said Petra. She turned to the others.

"I can raid my mother's candy stash. She always buys extra at Halloween. She will never miss it," said Maddox.

"I can request my mother to purchase sodas for our

drinking pleasure," said Sharming.

"*Our drinking pleasure.* I can't believe you just said that," laughed Jackie.

"What is wrong with that? Do you not want sodas?" Sharming always became formal when he was unsure of something.

"Nothing is wrong with that," said Billy. "Jackie is just being an ass." He mock-punched Jackie on the shoulder. "Now if that is all, then let's get ready." No one said anything. "We will meet at the base of the maple. I want all of our stuff up on the platform before the sun goes down. That means we should start by 8. Agreed?" Everyone nodded. Billy jumped to his feet. "Let's go get our stuff ready." Everyone headed to their respective houses to pack.

Jackie reached up and grabbed Billy by the arm. He mouthed the word, "Wait." He and Billy walked together. Jackie did not speak until everyone else was out of sight. "Billy Boy, do you think we could borrow a bit of power from Mrs. Cooper? Not a lot. In fact, it would not cost more than a few cents."

"Power?" responded Billy.

"I want to run an electrical cord from the shed up to the tree house. I checked out the cords my dad uses for the electric trimmer and I think they will reach."

"What do you need power for? I don't want the tree house lit up like a Christmas tree. Someone would be sure to see it, and poof," Billy snapped his fingers on both hands in Jackie's face, "our secret hideout would not be a secret anymore. Even our use of flashlights must be limited."

"Not lights. I want power for this." He slipped the backpack off his back and removed a surveillance camera. He held it out in front of Billy's face. I have my dad's old clunky laptop to record what this baby sees but they both need power. The battery on the laptop lasts about five minutes, so it has to be plugged in all the time." Billy stared back at him. Jackie moved the camera in front of Billy's face in what he thought was a hypnotic motion.

Finally, Billy reached up and grabbed his hand. "You want to record us up there. What for?"

"Billy Boy, sometimes I think you have a brain the size of a pea. We are going to gather evidence to take to the police. We mount this up in the cedar tree. I set it to detect motion. It will record whatever it sees happen on the freeway. If those fake cops come by again and hijack another truck, we will record them on the laptop. This baby has night vision."

"It looks pretty old and clunky."

"Don't let its looks deceive you. My dad got six of these

off of an auction site. They were used to surveil a large lumberyard, so they can see a long way at night. He was going to set them up in our yard, but he hasn't gotten around to it yet. We will borrow this one."

"Are you sure it will work?"

"Pretty sure I can make it work. It's not wireless or anything, but that just means it will be easier to make work. All we need is power." He gave Billy his most pleading look.

"Okay. Let's set it up. What else do you need besides extension cords?"

"Not much. Just a couple of screws to attach it to the tree. We should try to conceal the cord if we can. I have an orange cord that will go from the shed to the base of the tree. I want a black one to go up the tree, so no one will notice it."

"When do you want to do this?"

"Tomorrow after everyone leaves the fort."

Billy was warming to the idea of spying on the hijackers. He nodded. "Tomorrow." They walked home to pack for their campout in the secret hideout. Billy's mind wandered to all the secrets he was keeping. The camera would be just one more.

THE
SLEEP
OUT

It took 30 minutes to haul everyone's stuff up to the platform. There was only one incident. The paper bag containing all the sodas that Sharming's mom had donated to their sleepover, broke open halfway up when Maddox jerked too hard on the rope. The entire 24 cans of soda fell to the ground. Most were rescued but the first can, opened by Orph, sprayed all over her face. Everyone laughed hysterically. After that, everyone was careful and waited before opening theirs.

They played cards and ate until midnight. There was no agreement to stop. They all just drifted off to sleep. Everyone except Billy was sound asleep. He had to get up and shake the peanut shells out of his sleeping bag. He knew Jackie had been eating the peanuts and had tossed all the shells over his shoulder right into everyone's sleeping bag. It seemed no one cared except Billy. After emptying his sleeping bag, he tried to settle down and sleep. He stared out a knot hole at floor level. There was not much traffic on the freeway. Once a police car zoomed past with its lights flashing. It was soon followed by an ambulance. The lights were flashing, but the siren was off. Billy just figured there was an accident somewhere. He closed his eyes and did not open them again until a crow on a branch far up the tree started cawing. It was very early. He looked around. Everyone was asleep, with the exception of Petra. Her sleeping bag was empty.

Panic swelled up in Billy. He was instantly alert. He feared that something bad had happened. He looked over the railing and scanned Mrs. Cooper's backyard. He could not see her. He looked toward the freeway. The traffic was building for the morning rush. He looked back at the Cooper house just as a white van pulled into the Cooper yard.

Billy's panic increased, and he instinctively ducked down. Sharma woke and sat up. He yawned loudly. Billy shushed him and pointed down at the van in the Cooper yard. The rest of the gang was stirring. Billy and Sharma set about shushing the rest. Soon they were all laying on their bellies peeking through the cracks of the railing.

Orph tapped Billy on the shoulder and mouthed, "Where

is Petra?" Billy answered with a shrug of his shoulders. The van doors opened, and a man got out and opened the side door. He lifted a device the size of a small suitcase out of the van and set it on the ground. He returned to the van and came back with a wand-like device. He bent down and started to connect a series of cables to the device on the ground. Just then, Orph poked Billy and pointed at the back of the shed. A piece of toilet paper was fluttering up and down. Petra poked her head out. Billy sat up, so she could see him above the railing and waved her back. She ducked out of sight.

Jackie whispered, "It's a metal and depth detector. Really high end." The man carried the device by a handle to the front of the shed, turned it on and began to sweep the wand over the ground. The device hummed loudly. "He is looking for something. He is going right over the spot where you found the body."

Orph butted in, "You found a body!" She practically shouted, and the man stopped and looked around for the source of the voice. He seemed unsure if had heard anything over the noise of the machine.

Jackie hit her on the arm with the back of his hand, "Shhhh up," he mouthed, "or he will find us."

Billy turned to Orph and the others and whispered, "I'll

tell you later." He turned back to the man in the yard. He continued to sweep the metal detector over the ground, soon completing the section where the skeleton was found and proceeded to an area further away from the shed. After a few minutes, there was a loud squeal from the device. He stopped and set down the wand. He reached into his back pocket, pulled out a bunch of small sticks with triangular flags on the end. He stuck one in the ground and continued to scan. He continued this process three more times. After about 15 minutes—which seemed like a thousand years to the gang in the tree house—he stopped and looked at his watch. He disconnected the wand from the suitcase device and returned them both to the van. Returning with a small shiny shovel, he started to dig around each of the flags he had set in the ground. The gang watched and wondered.

Sharma touched Billy and whispered, "I must urinate very soon."

Maddox tapped him on the shoulder with an empty plastic soda bottle and pointed to the other side of the platform. He whispered, "Pee over there and don't make any noise."

Sharma took the bottle and crawled over to the far side of the platform. No one looked in his direction. They were all staring at the man on the ground who was on his knees, reaching his gloved hands into the hole he had dug. He soon came up with something. He held it up to the light and inspected it. "It's an old rusty lag screw," whispered Jackie.

They continued to watch the man as he dug at the other three flag locations. Every few minutes Petra would stick out her head and raise her hands. She was pleading for information on what was going on in the yard but the only response she got was instructions to remain hidden.

The man pulled two more pieces of metal from the ground. One was a spike and the other was a large rusty washer. The man started on the last flag. He had to dig deeper than before. Finally, he set down the shovel and reach into the hole. His hand came up holding something quite large, barely fitting in his hand. He flopped down to a sitting position and scraped away at the surface of the object. He removed his gloves, spit on what was in his hand and rubbed it with his finger. He spoke for the first time. "Yes!" he said and pumped his fist.

Billy looked at the object in the man's hand. It sort of looked like one of the brass figurines he had seen in the cellar of the Cooper place. The man stood up and filled all the holes with his shovel, tamped them down, walked to the van, and drove away. Billy automatically looked over in the direction where he had last seen Petra. Her head peeked out. He shouted from the tree fort, "All clear!"

Petra stepped from behind the garden shed. She had a roll of toilet paper in her hand with a meter hanging off of it. She tossed it in the air and then ran under it and caught it as she headed in the direction of the cedar tree. "I had to go," she announced, "and I didn't want to use a container, so I climbed down and peed behind the shed."

She reached the base of the tree, put on her safety belt and was about to climb up when Orph shouted down, "Stay there. I am coming down first. My bladder is about to burst." She climbed down the tree and was quickly followed by the rest of the gang, carrying their backpacks filled with a lot of empty snack packages. They left their sleeping bags and pillows on the platform. Only Jackie and Billy were left on the tree fort.

Petra called up, "Who was that?"

Billy glanced at Jackie who was about to explain about the skeleton Billy had found in the yard, so he nudged him. "Just someone from the university. My dad told them they could scan the yard for old metal objects," he said. It was not a lie. After retrieving the body, they looked into the history of the place and thought there might be some buried artifacts. He did not mention the skeleton he found.

Orph seemed to have forgotten about Jackie's earlier comment.

"Oh," said Petra, seemingly satisfied with the explanation. "Chuck the stuff down," she commanded. Jackie started tossing the rolled up sleeping bags and pillows over the top of the fort wall. There was a mad melee of the gang running around, trying to catch their stuff before it hit the ground. They were screaming with laughter. Billy and Jackie were last. Everyone gathered up all the camping equipment, climbed onto the shed, into the maple tree, and down to the lawn in the corner of the Beechwood Estates. It was early, and no one noticed them as they headed to their respective houses.

Jackie and Billy agreed to meet later that day to mount the surveillance camera high up in the cedar tree.

Mounting the camera, running the power cord, and setting up the old laptop to record took Jackie and Billy most of the afternoon. The sky had clouded over, and the rumbles of a threatening summer thunderstorm had kept any witnesses to their activities hidden away in their houses. It took them over an hour to program the camera to come on after dark and record only when motion was detected. "You know we are going to have to check whatever it records and fine-tune the sensitivity," said Jackie.

"I won't be able to check tomorrow. I'm going to the university with my dad. The scientists are going to tell us what they've found out about the skeleton, so it will have to be Monday after work. I have to finish scraping all that flaking paint off," said Billy, pointing to the house. "You want to help?"

"Naw. I don't do scraping," said Jackie. "Maybe I will check it out while you are out with your dad."

Jackie began to climb down from the tree fort. He was wearing his safety belt but neglected to clip on to the makeshift pitons they had installed for safety. Billy stopped him. "Get used to using the carabiners," he said.

"Sorry, I forgot," said Jackie, climbing down from the tree fort, clipping onto the screw-eye pitons as he went.

A
VISIT
TO
THE
UNIVERSITY

CHAPTER 17

The next day Billy and his dad headed to the university with a brief stop at the police station to drop off the tent that had been left on the Cooper property. While his dad was talking to the officer at the desk, Billy wandered. He looked at a series of bulletin boards with various posters ranging from a play being presented by the local theatre group to pictures of previously stolen bicycles recovered by the police. On one board there was a series of pictures with the heading "Most Wanted." Billy scanned from picture to picture. He shivered as he looked at what appeared to be very nasty people. He muttered to himself, "I wonder if any of these guys are one of those fake cops hijacking trucks?" He realized he'd said the last few words out loud.

"Fake what?" asked his dad, having just finished at the desk.

"What?" said Billy.

"You were mumbling something about fake cops."

Billy felt his face flush. "Nothing, Dad. I was just looking at those pictures of criminals. I sure wouldn't want to meet any of them in a dark alley," he said and smiled in an effort to deflect his dad from the topic of fake cops.

His dad looked at them. He pointed his finger at one with an ugly skull tattoo on his neck. "This guy looks especially nasty." Billy nodded. "We have to drive around back to one of the storage sheds to drop off the tent." With that, he walked out of the police station.

A few minutes later, they were heading up the hill to the university. They parked and made their way to the archeology labs and offices. "Your mother used to go here before you were born. She took some English courses and at least one archeology course. I remember picking her up over at the dorms." He pointed across the campus. "I must admit I am interested in that body. It is not every day you find a skeleton." He looked at Billy. "You don't seem very excited about this. What is it with you? I thought you would be interested in finding out what they have discovered. You're not scared, are you? It was just some old bones."

"Sorry. I was just thinking that the skeleton had a name. Do you think they figured out his name?"

His dad reached for the door and pulled it open. "Let's go and see, shall we."

They walked down two flights of stairs and looked down a long hallway. The light was not very bright. To Billy it looked a little like a movie where the unsuspecting heroes walked right into a laboratory filled with half-rotten zombies. They turned a corner and walked right into a man wearing a light-green lab coat. Billy recognized him as the man who had used the metal detector at the Cooper place. He said nothing. Billy's father held out his hand, "Braithwaite—Matt Braithwaite, and this is Billy. We're here about the skeleton found on the Cooper property."

"Hi," said the man. "I have been expecting you. Come in. I'm Upton—Ed Upton."

Billy and his dad walked into a brightly lit room with an office to one side. There were tables with various tools spread out on them. Some had rocks half chipped apart while others had bones that had been cut with one of the saws. There was one table completely covered with a cloth. It appeared to be covering the skeleton.

"Forgive the mess. This is our workshop."

"Are you a doctor?" asked Billy.

"Not yet," said Ed. "I'm still studying to get my doctorate. I am really interested in that guy over there. He has been telling me some very interesting stories." Billy looked puzzled. Ed walked over and pulled the sheet off with a flourish. "This is Mr. Wong. That is not his real name. I named him that because I think he is—or was—Chinese."

"How can you tell?" asked Billy's father.

Ed reached down and picked up the skull and turned it upside down. He ran his finger along the jawbone and teeth, a few of which were missing. "This is his palate. I noticed that the curve of the jaw is rather elliptical. It is more common for persons of Asian ethnicity to have curved jawbones, while people of Caucasian decent are more parabolic." He looked at his audiences and realized that neither Billy or his father understood what he was saying. He walked over to a cupboard, reached in and pulled out another skull. He carried it over to the skeleton. "Look. Compare these two." He held them out, teeth up with the lower-jaw removed. "See how this one is shorter and less pointy than this one? Well, that is one of the reasons I think this man was Asian. Also, this." He reached into his pocket and pulled out a small green object. It was intricately carved. "I found this stuck to one of his ribs. It probably was around his neck when he died. I thought it was a rock at first, but once I cleaned it up I saw it was a jade dragon pendant. I am pretty sure it was a symbol used by a Chinese gang in this area in 1880 to about 1910. They were mostly thieves. Little is known about their leadership, but the archives refer to precious metal and jewel thieves that plied their trade in this area. They would steal gold from miners and silver objects from local households, melt them down, and cast the metal inside hollow brass trinkets or small gold bars. Most of the booty ended back in China."

"Cool," said Billy as he reached for the jade dragon pendant.

"It is very fragile, so be careful," said Ed, handing him the pendant. Billy turned it in his hands, inspected it thoughtfully, and handed it back to Ed. "Oh, and I almost forgot. I took the liberty of scanning around the old grave with a metal detector and I found this. He went to the cupboard and pulled out a brass creature about the size of Billy's fist. A two-headed brass figure that looked like a bear and a pig. It's hollow." He turned it upside down and showed the hole in the bottom. "According to the archives, the thieves would melt down the precious metals they stole, pour it inside a brass creature like this, and then close the hole with a brass plug. The final result would look like a solid brass object."

"That is very interesting," said Billy's dad. "There is an old forge in the cellar of the Cooper place. And, if I remember correctly, there were a few brass creatures on one of the shelves in there. You don't suppose the Cooper place was where they did this casting?"

Ed Upton suddenly became very excited. "May I come and see this forge? It might fill in a lot of blanks in a very old mystery concerning what happened to all the treasure that was stolen over nearly 30-years. How old is the house?"

"I don't really know, but I have found and removed wiring that is over a hundred years old. So, I suppose—"

"Are you there this week?" Ed asked. "I have no time until later in the week. Perhaps, Thursday, in the afternoon?"

"One of us is sure to be there. Billy here has a lot of scraping to do." He grinned and nudged Billy.

Billy rolled his eyes.

"See you then," his Dad said. "And thanks for the education."

They turned to go. Billy turned back suddenly. "Wait—did you find out how Mr. Wong died?"

Upton walked over and picked up the skull, holding it up. His index finger was inside a hole in the skull. Billy could see the finger through the eye socket, wiggling back and forth. "Your guess is as good as mine," said Ed with a grin, "but I'm thinking this had something to do with it."

He tossed what looked like a small rock from hand to hand. "It's likely a bullet—or *was* a bullet. I haven't researched it yet."

As they walked out of the building, Billy realized that Mr. Wong had probably been murdered. That was not what frightened him. It was the visit planned by Ed Upton. He would explore the cellar and maybe he would find the shelf that opened into the bricked-up tunnel. That would lead him to the shed, and the tunnel under the freeway, and then everyone would know about it before he could explore it properly. It was *his* secret. If there was any treasure, he wanted to find it. It was his discovery, and he didn't want anyone to take it away from him. On Monday, when his dad was out on an errand, he would go down into the cellar and hide the wire that opened the cubbies. Maybe he would borrow his dad's screw gun and make sure it didn't open at all. The need to keep it all a secret overwhelmed him to the point where he no longer felt like talking to anyone in case it all came out in a guilty rush.

GETTING READY TO EXPLORE

Monday morning, Billy woke up early. His sleep had been restless, but he woke with a plan. He shoved two LED flashlights into his pocket, along with a strap that fit around his head. The flashlights were designed to fit into the strap. It was his geek light.

He realized that his dad would have to climb under the section of the house where the bricked tunnel started, too, at the very least, to check the foundation. What better place to get under the house than to go through the wall behind the shelf? It was only a matter of time before someone found the tunnel. They would take over and he, William Braithwaite, would be pushed out. The archeologist guys at the university would be crawling over everything. He slid his hand to the belt buckle still in his pocket. He had considered giving it to Ed Upton. But he did not. He wondered why, then answered his own question. It was part of his secret. It would remain his until he found out whatever there was to find out, and only then would he share it with the archeologists.

In order to do that, he must get busy. He would lock off the cellar entrance by screwing the shelf closed. That would probably keep Ed Upton from discovering the tunnel. His dad would not get to the foundation inspection for at least two weeks, probably three. That gave him some time.

Billy poured cereal into a bowl, sloshed it with milk that he had smelled first to make sure it was not sour, and sat at the table. In front of him were three postcards sent from various countries in Europe. They were from his mother and sister. They were not due home for at least a month. There wasn't much written. His mother said she hoped everything was running smoothly at home; they were having a marvelous time; and they wished Billy and his dad were there. On the bottom of the card his sister had printed,

Hey, William,

IGYNH—SOOMROIWKY

Your loving sister

Billy grinned as he translated his sister's code. This first part said, "I'm glad you're not here," to which Billy responded aloud, "The feeling is mutual."

His dad entered the kitchen. "Oh, I see you found the postcards from your mother and sister. I hope you know what that code at the bottom means because I have no idea." He looked expectantly at Billy for a translation.

Billy did not want to get his sister in trouble. Not because he cared, but because he figured she had more on him than he had on her. Best not to tattle. "I have no idea. She is just being her weird self. You will have to ask her when she gets home." It was partially true. It wasn't until *after* his father asked what it meant that he translated the last section to read, "Stay out of my room or I will kill you." This made Billy instantly curious. He wondered, *What has she got in there that she wants kept secret?* He grinned again. If she had never mentioned going into her room, he would never have thought of it, but now he knew he would have to sneak in and have a little look around.

His dad interrupted his thoughts. "How is the paint scraping coming?"

"Good," Billy replied. "I'll need a couple more days."

"The wood stain is in the kitchen. It's latex, so be sure you clean the used brushes with water."

"You mean I have to paint it, too?"

"Yep."

"Aw, Dad."

"Don't whine. It detracts from your character."

"Whatever that means," said Billy under his breath.

"Finish up, and let's go. I'll drop you off. I have a concrete truck scheduled at 8:30 for the Herbert's new driveway. I doubt I'll be back until lunch."

Billy lifted the bowl, slurping back the remaining cereal and milk. He wiped his mouth on his sleeve and grabbed an apple and two pieces of leftover pizza. He stuffed them in a plastic bag and followed his dad out to the truck. "You don't have to worry about lunch. I have enough here to take me till mid-afternoon. Take your time and finish the job."

His father looked at him, smiled and said, "Now that's how a responsible young man plans. I really appreciate you thinking of me and the job instead of just yourself."

Billy blushed. Not because he felt the praise but because he had an ulterior motive. He needed a least a couple of extra hours to explore further down the tunnel. He muttered, "Thanks, Dad," as the truck pulled into the Cooper driveway and he jumped out.

Billy watched his father drive away. He looked at the scraping job and realized he needed to speed things up to get some extra time to explore. He jogged to the house, grabbed the tools, and started scraping. Two hours later, he grabbed the apple from his bag and stuffed it into his mouth. He ate it without stopping his job. By noon, he realized that he had nearly finished the entire job. There was only a two-meter section left at the back of the house. He stopped. He would leave this as something to come back to when his father arrived. It would appear as if he had never stopped.

Billy knew there was deception involved but finding out what was at the other end of the tunnel had become all-consuming. He grabbed a piece of cold pizza and headed to the shed with the ladder under his arm. He quickly inserted the metal bar into the slot in the floor and pulled. The trapdoor creaked open. He removed the lever and tucked it beside one of the wall studs, then slid the step-ladder into the hole. He was about to step down when he remembered the creak. Glancing at the shelf on the other side of the room, he saw an oil can, the kind with a thumb lever that squirts oil out a nozzle. Beside it, was a funny looking, two-headed rock hammer, with a point at one side and a flat section on the other. He grabbed them both and climbed down. At the bottom, he fitted one of his flashlights into the head strap and turned it on, then stuck the rock hammer into his belt. His plan was to close the door behind him, so no one would know where he went.

And he did not want it to creak when he opened it back up. He moved the ladder over to the spring mechanism that reminded him of a pair of garage door springs. He squirted oil all over the moving parts, then reached up and pulled the trapdoor closed. When he pulled the lever on the wall, the trapdoor opened again with much less squeaking and creaking. He oiled some more and repeated the process until the trapdoor opened with only a soft thud. After pulling it closed again, he headed down the tunnel with a mouthful of pizza, a rock hammer dangling from his belt, and one of his LED flashlights pointing down the tunnel.

EXPLORING THE TUNNEL

Billy felt a shiver run down his spine. He was a real explorer. The unknown was unfolding in front of him. New mysteries were his to explore and solve. Who knew if he would find gold and jewels, or other treasure, at the end of the tunnel. He entered the narrow tunnel that sloped gently down. This time he inspected the support beams as he went. If they were rotten he needed to know. He looked at the first post and noticed that it was set on a rock pillar that kept it from touching the wet ground. He looked up at a support beam set on top of two posts on either side of the tunnel. The tops of the posts were covered with thick roofing material. The beam was dripping black. Billy reached up to touch the beam just a few centimeters above his head. It was shiny black, but dry, and completely coated in tar. That would keep it from rotting for a very long time. Billy realized that whoever built the tunnel wanted it to last for a long time and never be accidentally discovered.

He continued down the slope to the section of solid wet rock walls he had reached before the day his flashlight went dead. The new LED lights would last at least ten times as long, and he had two of them. He felt secure that they would provide him with all the light he needed. He walked down the tunnel. It was colder and wetter the further he traveled. The ceiling got closer to his head until he had to duck to avoid scraping his head on the rock above. After a few meters, the rock became smoother on the walls and ceiling. Billy could see where the wall of a natural tunnel had been cut away to provide access. The ceiling was now covered with small, newly-formed stalactites. They were forming on the remnants of older larger stalactites that had been broken off. There were shards along the edge of the floor where it curved up to form the walls.

Billy continued down the natural tunnel past the point he had previously turned back. It continued to slope down and narrowed. He ran his hands along both tunnel walls as he went. He occasionally felt a vibration, and realized he was probably right under the freeway. The floor leveled out, and he continued for another 15-meters. The vibrations stopped, and the floor of the tunnel began to gradually slope upwards and narrowed until he felt his shoulders brushing the sides as he walked. In the distance he could only see a wall of rock. *It's a dead end,* he thought. Billy began to feel claustrophobic. He'd never felt that way before, so he wasn't exactly sure why he felt that way now, but it probably had something to do with the walls closing in on him. Although it was cool, he began to sweat under his t-shirt. He felt an urge to turn around and run back to the light—and the ladder leading to safety. "Just a few more steps," he whispered. "Don't be a fraidy cat," he said out loud. He took another few steps, all the while staring at what looked like an end wall. He shook his head back and forth. He was saying "no" to going forward. The act caused the geek light to wave back and forth with the motion of his head. The beam seemed to lengthen when it hit the left side of the end of the tunnel.

"You are an idiot. The tunnel doesn't end. It just bends to the left." He quickened his pace and soon reached the section of the tunnel where it sloped up and to the left. He looked in that direction and frowned. Moving a bit closer, he saw a barred gate three-meters in front of him. He inspected it more closely and discovered a metal frame of flat bars set into the rock on both sides and the ceiling of the tunnel. A barred gate was hinged to the frame. A large lock hung on a hasp attached to the far side of the gate. The bars were rusted iron but still held strong. The lock was half concealed by a flat, iron frame. Billy reached through the bars and rattled the lock. It was big and solid. It had a slight green tinge and looked like it was made of brass. It was locked.

He took the rock hammer from his belt and tried to reach through the bars and hit the lock. He hoped it was old enough to break open. After a number of tries, he stopped. The sweat was pouring down his face. It was impossible to hit the lock with a solid blow from this side of the barred gate. He inspected the iron frame that held the gate. Maybe he could break it free from the rock. He started to hammer at the rock face. He stopped when a small shard spit out and stung his cheek. He sat down and stared at the gate. Someone sure did not want anyone to use this tunnel. It was obvious to Billy that the lock on the outside meant that someone with a key would come in the tunnel, drop something off, or pick something up, and leave again. They would not stay because the gate could only be locked from the outside. The fact that they had a locking gate in a secret tunnel meant they would not leave it unlocked for any length of time.

Billy stood up and slipped the hammer back into his belt, turned around and headed back to the shed. His sense of claustrophobia where the tunnel narrowed did not bother him as much on the return trip. He reached the ladder, climbed up and out, and pulled the ladder after him, then closed the trapdoor. He was about to drag the ladder back to the front porch when he decided he could just leave it where it was leaning against the wall in the shed. It might look suspicious dragging a ladder into the shed and then disappearing. He could tell his dad that he thought it was better to store the ladder in the shed instead of the front porch. Some passerby might see it and decide to take it. He headed back to the house to finish scraping the last small section of old paint. His father did not show up until he was finished and then could only stay for a few minutes.

"No point in starting to paint this late. You can have the rest of the day off. I will drop you at home," his dad said. "By the way, nice job so far." He grinned. "I'll make a 'jack-of-all-trades' out of you yet." He leaned down and looked closer at Billy's face. He pointed at his cheek. "What happened there? Looks like you have been bleeding."

Billy touched his cheek and felt where the shard of rock had hit his face. He stuck his finger in his mouth and then rubbed spit on the scratch. "Something hit me while I was working. It's nothing."

"I'll get you some safety glasses. That could have hit

you in the eye," grunted his father. "Remind me."

Billy nodded and climbed into the truck.

no more surveillance

CHAPTER 20

As they approached the house they could see Jackie sitting on the porch. "Looks like your friend is waiting. How did he know you were getting off early?" asked Billy's dad.

"Dunno," mumbled Billy.

"Proper English, please. You talk like that when your mother gets home, and I will be the one in trouble," said his father.

"I don't know. Maybe he was going to wait all day. Jackie is pretty weird. It's something he would do," replied Billy. He opened the door of the truck and jumped out. "See you later, Dad." The truck sped away as Billy strolled up to Jackie. "Are you waiting for me?"

"NO. I just like sitting on your porch. I have found that it is the best spot in the universe to reflect on the nature of existence," he said, the words dripping with sarcasm.

"Who else would I be waiting for?"

Billy sat down. "Whatcha want to do?"

"It is no longer what I *want* to do but what I *have* to do."

"Then what is it you *have* to do?"

Jackie stood up, picked up a rock, and threw it down the driveway. "My dad, all of a sudden, wants to install the cameras that he's had in the basement for half a century. He counted them and noticed one was missing. He came straight to my room without even "passing Go" and started yelling at me. I tried to ask him why he did not ask my sister first. Her room was closer. But that just made him angrier. I tried to explain why I had borrowed it, but he didn't want to listen. He said if the camera and old laptop were not back before he got home from work I could kiss the rest of the summer goodbye."

Billy stood up, "You didn't tell him about the hijackers, did you?"

"No! *What do you take me for?* I tried to tell him that our fort needed surveillance, but he was not interested. I even felt it was sort of the truth. We did need it for surveillance." He sighed. "Anyway, I have to get the camera out of the tree and back in the basement before 5:30—when my dad gets home." Jackie threw another rock. "And *that* is why I'm on your porch waiting for you. We need to get your dad's screw gun, climb up to the fort, and disconnect the whole thing. So where is the screw gun?"

"My dad left his tools in the Cooper house. Let's go," said Billy. Jumping to his feet, he hurried towards the old maple tree. Jackie followed. "I will go first, and you keep an eye out for observers. Once I am in the tree, I will signal you when the coast is clear."

A few minutes later, they were both on the large branch that hung over the fence above the shed on the Cooper property. They dropped down onto the roof and climbed down the pallet leaning up against the end wall. Billy went to the backdoor of the house, lifted a rock near the steps, picked up a key, and went into the house. A few minutes later, he returned with the screw gun in hand. Jackie was coming out of the shed with their safety harnesses. He pulled a cloth shopping bag out of his back pocket. "Put the screw gun in this. I brought it to carry the camera and the laptop. We can use the rope to lower them down." They slipped into their homemade climbing harnesses and ascended the tree to the platform of the tree house. It took only a few minutes to remove the camera.

"Let's look at the footage and see if we got anything," said Jackie. He opened the laptop. There were about fifty video files on the desktop. "Crap," swore Jackie. "We don't have time to look at all of these. I bet each shows a car driving past. Great intel: fifty cars drove past between midnight and 4:00 a.m."

Billy looked at the files. "Open that one," he ordered.

"What is so special about that one?"

"It is longer than the others. See the length. This one is huge. It's 15-minutes long. Everything else is like 10-seconds. Probably that is how long it takes a car to come into view and zoom past. Open that one. There was some movement for 15-minutes. That is about how long it would take to pull over a truck and hijack it."

"Nice catch, Billy Boy," said Jackie and he started the video. They watched in silence. A car came down the freeway very slowly. Smoke was coming out of the hood. It rolled to a stop on the side of the freeway. A man got out of the car, walked to the front, and stared at the vapor billowing out of the hood. He opened the hood and more vapor rose up. He went to the trunk of the car and opened it. He took out a jug of liquid and walked back to the front. He reached under the hood with his hand and pulled it back quickly. He was jumping up and down. It appeared as if he had burned his hand.

"The car over-heated. He will have to wait until the engine cools down before he can open the radiator cap and pour the liquid in. It is probably water. That is why this video is so long. It's not a hijacking; it's just a broken-down car," said Billy as he looked down at the freeway. "Look." He pointed. The car is still there.

Jackie glanced up at the car and back to the screen. "He is thumbing a ride from another car."

"What do you mean, *thumbing*?" asked Billy.

"Hitchhiking. You remember that old horror movie we watched at my birthday party? It was called *The Hitcher*. That young couple almost runs over a guy hitchhiking, so they pick him up and he tries to kill them about 500-times. It was hysterically funny."

"Oh," said Billy. He remembered the movie, but he also remembered closing his eyes and plugging his ears during the bloody parts. He was not going to tell Jackie that. He glanced back at the computer screen. The hitch-hiking man had been picked up. The video ended.

"I have to erase these. My dad will look at them if we leave them and he will wonder why they were taken from a height. That will cause him to ask questions." With that, he selected them all and hit the delete button. They all vanished. After unhooking everything, he put it all into the cloth bag. He tied the rope onto the bag and lowered it all down while Billy climbed down and untied the rope.

Once everything was back in place, they climbed onto the shed roof, into the maple tree, and headed back into the Glen.

"Catch you later," said Jackie as he veered off towards his house carrying the shopping bag of equipment.

"Yeah," said Billy. He was just about home when he remembered that they had left the electrical cord still up in the tree fort. He couldn't leave it there. It was like an arrow pointing to the secret fort. It had to come down. Besides, he could use it elsewhere. The tunnel would be far less frightening if it were lit. His dad had removed a lot of the old electrical light fixtures and piled them up in the living room of the Cooper place. Billy could rescue a few of them and hang them in the tunnel. But that was a job he could start tomorrow. He had to figure out a way of getting that big brass lock off the barred gate at the end of the tunnel.

LIGHTS AND VISITORS

CHAPTER 21

Billy's job the next morning was to paint the freshly-scraped siding. Billy started on the front of the house. His dad was still rewiring the kitchen. New recessed lighting was to be installed in the kitchen ceiling after the old warped wooden lath and plaster was removed. At one point, Billy was called to help drag the plaster debris out to the truck. He still finished applying the first coat of paint on the front of the house just before lunch.

They sat on the front stoop and ate the sandwiches his father had made. Not much was said until they had practically finished eating. "You miss your mum?" his dad asked suddenly.

Billy grinned. "Yeah. She makes better sandwiches than you. And she always gives me a treat. I don't see a treat in this bucket." He flipped the lid of the lunch-bucket closed.

"Yeah, I miss her too. She always gives me a treat too.

I am partial to her homemade cookies. She called me on Skype late last night after you had gone to bed. She asked after you. Said she missed you. They will be home in three weeks."

Billy nodded. He knew he was looking forward to seeing his mum but not so sure about his sister. Maybe she would be nicer after her trip around Europe. He hoped, but he also had his doubts.

"Well—back to work," said his dad. He admired Billy's painting job. Billy did too. He was a good painter; he'd found out last summer that he could not cut corners unless he wanted to do the job twice. "Excellent job, William. Only three more sides to go." He smiled and ruffled Billy's hair. "I have to go to the dump and then strip some forms from the driveway I poured last week. I will pick you up around 4:30." He turned to go and then quickly turned back. "What do you want for supper?"

"Ribs," said Billy without hesitation, "with chipotle BBQ sauce."

"Ribs it is," replied his dad, and he turned and left.

Billy was going to paint as much as he could in two hours, then grab some of the old light fixtures from the floor in the living room, remove the extension cords from the tree house, open the trapdoor, and run the cords down the tunnel as far as they would go. He might even get time to connect some of the fixtures. He painted as fast as he could. After two hours, he had a small section remaining. He stopped, planning to return to painting just before his father arrived. He wanted it to look like he had never stopped, that way no questions would be asked.

Billy climbed up into the tree fort, removed the extension cords, and dropped them to the ground. He and Jackie had run the cords from the shed to the base of the tree the long way around—along the fence separating the Glen from the Cooper property, in order to easily conceal them. There was a lot of cord. Hopefully, enough to go all the way to the barred gate in the tunnel. He coiled the individual cords up and carried them into the shed, then opened the trapdoor and dropped the ladder down. Separating the shortest cord, he set it on the bench. He would use this cord to plug into the cords that ran down the tunnel. It would be connected when he entered, and then removed when he left. That way he would not have to leave a telltale cord running across the floor when he was not here.

He had selected a half-dozen old fixtures with bulbs still screwed into their sockets. He carried the cords and all the lights down into the tunnel. Each fixture had the bare ends of wire from their previous connections. He straightened the stiff wires and prepared each for connection to the extension cords. He had watched his father do this many times. He shoved the stiff wire right into the slots of the multi-receptacle extension cord, taped them in place with electrical tape, and then plugged the next cord into another of the receptacles in the head. This way, he was able to create a string of lights. He heard his father's voice in his head, "This is not the safest way to do this, but it's quick and dirty. Never leave a contraption like this plugged in." Billy smiled. He liked the phrase "quick and dirty."

He soon had his six lights connected to the extension cords coiled on the floor of the cave. He climbed the ladder, plugged in the short cord, dropped it down, and proceeded to connect it to his *quick-and-dirty* light string. He squinted just before the plug made contact just in case the whole thing turned into a gigantic short circuit and he was showered with sparks, like a firework. All the lights worked except one. Bill jiggled the wires. It came on. He re-taped the connection. The string of lights would—fingers crossed—run along the floor of the cave all the way to the barred gate.

He stood admiring his work, then picked up the coil of lights, avoiding the now hot bulbs. He was about to walk down the tunnel, uncoiling as he went, when he heard a thump from above. He froze and waited. It sounded like a car door. He dropped the string of lights. One of the lights gave a little pop and went out. He ignored it. Bulbs could be replaced. He rushed back to the ladder and climbed up. He had just reached the top when he heard voices. "It doesn't look like there is anybody here," said a female voice.

"Good. I peeked into the house—front door was locked. Have a look in the shed," said a male voice that Billy though he had heard before but could not place.

"Okay, but we shouldn't trespass."

"We are already trespassing. Look in the damn shed."

Billy felt panic well up from his toes to his hair. It felt like his hair was standing straight up. He sucked air into his lungs and reacted. He grabbed the cord that was running from the workbench, across the floor and down to his string of lights. He pulled on it, in an effort to get the plug out of its receptacle above the workbench. It did not budge. He yanked harder and the cord came free. It rattled across the workbench and clunked to the floor. Billy pulled on the cord and it snaked down into the hole in the floor.

"What was that? I heard something," said a female voice just outside the shed door. Billy stepped higher on the ladder and pulled the handle on the trapdoor. It closed almost silently. The only noise he heard was the creaking hinges of the shed door as it was opened. He held his breath, crouching down on the top of the ladder, still clutching the trapdoor handle.

"There is nobody in here," said the male voice. "You imagined it. Probably a mouse or a rat."

"I hate rats."

"I was just teasing. There's no food around here, so probably not rats."

"Why would a painter leave their paint bucket and brush out to dry up, unless they were nearby and planned to return shortly?" Billy held his breath, listening intently. "Okay, let's just have a quick look around. I found that hollow brass figurine right here. According to the archives, there was a ring of thieves that belonged to one of the Chinese Triads that robbed gold miners when they came into town. Sometimes they concealed their booty inside brass creatures. They were never caught. In fact, there is a story that a bunch of miners got together and formed a vigilante group. They started a war with the Chinese gangsters and wiped them out. They searched for their gold but never found it. Only two figurines filled with gold, along with a box of small gold bars were ever found. And they were discovered on a ship bound for Hong Kong.

The rest of the gold was lost."

"And you think the gold was stashed somewhere around here?"

"Yeah. The guy that is fixing up this house told me there is a forge in the cellar of the house. I have an appointment to come and see it on Thursday, but I wanted to have a look around the property without having to explain what I was looking for."

Billy recognized the voice. It was the archeology graduate student from the university. He continued to listen. The man spoke again. "The body was found here by the kid. I suspect that Mr. Wong was killed and buried here. I found a bullet and compared it to the hole in Mr. Wong's skull. I am guessing someone murdered him. I also ran the metal detector over the yard and found that brass bear-pig thing over there somewhere. I figured there might be more, and perhaps some of them are filled with gold. You have a look over there. I will check near the edge of the property."

"What the heck am I looking for?" asked the woman.

"I have no idea, but if you see something out of the ordinary, like a hump or depression in the ground where one shouldn't be, let me know."

"What do we do if we find something?"

"Do you have any idea what gold is selling for these days? It's a lot. Wouldn't you like to pay off those student loans and maybe buy a car someday?"

"You mean keep it?" said the female voice. Billy imagined the man nodding his head. "Technically, it would belong to the government."

"It would be easy to smash away the brass containers, melt down the gold and sell it. It's not like anyone is looking for it after a hundred years. I'm a firm believer in "finders-keepers." Now go and look."

After a few minutes of waiting and not hearing any sounds, Billy pulled the lever to open the trapdoor. He was glad he had oiled the springs and hinges; the trapdoor opened with a soft, almost inaudible thump. He quickly climbed out and pushed the trapdoor closed behind him. He went to the small dirty window beside the door and peeked out. He could see the two people wandering over the far sections of the Cooper property. After about ten minutes, the girl yelled out, "There's nothing here! Let's go before someone comes."

"Okay. You want to come with me on Thursday when I get to see the forge? It might hold a clue or two." They walked to the white van and drove away.

Billy realized he was way behind on getting back to

painting before his dad arrived. He opened the trapdoor, pulled up the ladder, closed the door, and headed back to where he had left his painting materials and tools. No sooner had he picked up his brush than his father arrived. The truck pulled right up beside him. "Not as fast as this morning, eh? That's okay—it's better to do a good job than rush and have to do a re-do. Clean up and we can head to the supermarket to buy some of those baby-back ribs you like so much."

Billy grinned and shoved the brush in a container of water, then resealed the tin of paint. He jumped in the truck with his mind racing. His thoughts were rushing down the tunnel to the barred gate. If there was gold on the other side, then he was going to be the one to discover it. He was going to tell his dad about the visitors but immediately realized that would expose all his plans. He was silent on the way to the supermarket while his dad rambled about the concrete driveway job.

PRISON VISIT

CHAPTER 22

That evening, Billy and his dad gorged themselves on ribs. Billy loved it when his dad cooked ribs. There was never a vegetable to be seen. Just ribs—piles of ribs. If his mother were here, he would be required to eat a vegetable, but she was not, so they put on bibs and ate sticky ribs until they could barely move. They looked at the pile of bones on the table and the sauce all over their hands and faces and started to laugh.

Later, Billy lay in bed. Every few minutes he had to sit up and burp because he had washed it all down with a gigantic bottle of soda. He smiled because that was another thing that his mother would frown upon. He could hear her voice in his head, "One glass of soda has enough sugar to last a person for a week."

Despite all the pleasure the dinner had given him, he still missed his mum. He missed her giggles when his dad would smack her on the bum at breakfast time. He missed blueberry pancakes and raisin-chocolate-chip cookies, but most of all he missed her coming into his room and kissing his forehead right before he fell asleep.

Billy could feel her touch, even if she wasn't there. He fell asleep. He dreamed....

He was hiding in the tunnel while zombies wandered the yard of the Cooper place. His mind welled with the need to escape through the tunnel and out the barred-gate at the end. It was the only way out. The shed was filling with the undead, slowly wandering and bumping into each other, moaning and hissing with each contact. But the gate was locked with a huge brass padlock. The floor above his head was creaking with the weight of dozens of rotting corpses. More were squeezing into the shed with each passing second. The cracks in the floor were leaking zombie guts. A drop of disgusting fluid fell through a crack and nearly hit Billy in the eye. The smell made his stomach heave. The floor was about to break under all the weight. Billy ran down the tunnel just as the floor collapsed. The zombies in the yard heard the crash and were attracted to the noise. They turned to the shed and fell through the broken floor on top of the dismembered bodies of undead. They continued to fill the tunnel, gradually lurching down towards the locked gate where Billy crouched. He tried to be quiet, hoping they would not notice him, but the smell made him gag. He put his hand over his mouth just as a zombie was about to touch him with a boney hand. He woke up suddenly, slipped out of bed, and ran to the bathroom. He felt like he was about to puke. He stuck his head over the toilet, but nothing came out. His stomach slowly settled. He got a drink of water and rinsed his mouth. He walked back to bed and pulled the covers up to his ears. His last thought before he fell asleep was *I have to find a way to open the lock at the end of the tunnel.*

The next two days were spent painting and wondering about the grad-students visit to the forge on Thursday. Billy had reentered the cellar with his dad's screw gun and made sure that the university students coming to inspect the forge would not discover the tunnel. He had replaced the blown bulb on his string of lights and run the cords all the way down the tunnel to the locked gate. He even drilled a hole in a concealed area of the shed floor at the end of the work bench and threaded the extension cord down to his string of lights. He could now keep the trapdoor closed when he was in the tunnel.

After dinner, Billy decided he would go and visit Jackie. He had been grounded for the camera/computer fiasco.

Billy slipped down the driveway to the back of Jackie's house. He had a handful of pebbles that he proceeded to toss at Jackie's bedroom window. After the third one hit with a resounding 'tink', Jackie opened his window. He had a big smile on his face. He whispered down at Billy, "It's about fracking time. They won't let me use the phone, and I have to be in my room after supper. I need to talk to a real human being—get up here."

"Are you allowed to have visitors?"

"It never came up, so I'll assume I can." Jackie winked. "But to be on the safe side, come in the basement door, and go all the way upstairs. They are watching the news and won't hear you."

"Are you sure?"

"It's better to ask—"

"...for forgiveness than for permission. I know. On my way," said Billy, and he disappeared from Jackie's view. A minute later, he slipped into Jackie's room.

"Am I ever glad to see you. I have been going *nutso*."

"How long are you in jail for?"

"After today, I will have nine days left. I am not sure I can do the time." He sighed and flopped down on his bed. "Tell me what you have been up to—in detail."

"Nothing much. Just working at the Cooper place."

"How was the trip to the university?"

"Boring. Except for finding out that the skeleton was a Chinese man. The guys at the university named him Mr. Wong. They think he was murdered. He had a hole in his skull. He was shot in the head."

"Cool. It sounds like he was executed. How long ago did he die?

"They figure about a 100 years ago."

"Do they know who killed him?"

"Nah," said Billy. He slipped his hand into his pocket and without considering the consequences he pulled out the buckle and flipped it in the air. On the second flip Jackie quickly sat up and snatched the buckle out of the air.

"Give it back," insisted Billy, feeling stupid for taking it out in the first place.

Jackie inspected the buckle. "As I recall, there were some doodles you asked me to figure out."

Billy snatched the buckle back. "I never asked you to do anything. Last time you spit on my buckle. That was not cool. I don't want you to spit on it again," shouted Billy.

"I wasn't going to spit on it."

"What were you going to do?"

"I was going to dirty it up. You know, rub some dirt or soot into the little cracks, accentuate whatever it says, so we can read it," responded Jackie defensively.

"It doesn't say anything. Just some scratches from being so old, that's all." Billy slipped it back into his pocket.

They both heard a shout from the hallway. It was Jackie's sister. "Mom, Dad, the cretin has somebody in his room. That is *not* allowed. You wouldn't let me have any visitors when I was grounded."

"Crap," he said as he jumped off his bed and went to the door. He opened it and shouted out, "You weren't allowed visitors because that was the reason you were grounded in the first place: visitors—boy type visitors. No one said I couldn't have visitors, and anyway Billy doesn't count. We are brothers." He slammed the door to his bedroom.

A few seconds later, there was a tap at his door and his mother poked her head inside. "Time to go home, Billy. Jackie, the lawyer, is grounded. He is not allowed visitors."

Jackie started to whine, "But you never said—"

His mother held her hand up. "I don't have to. I am the boss of you, and I can make up rules as I go. Maybe next time you will *ask* permission before you act."

Billy walked toward the door and past Jackie's mum, "Sorry, Mrs. Houston." He left the room and walked home. He was thinking about Jackie's suggestion of making the buckle dirty, so he could make out the worn markings. He would light a candle over a piece of aluminum foil and rub the resulting soot into the cracks. Maybe then he could decipher the etchings on the buckle's edges.

UNIVERSITY VISITORS

Thursday morning found Billy in the Cooper house living room. His dad had smashed all the old plaster off the walls with a sledge hammer and a spade. Under the plaster were thin strips of wood called lath and bits of chicken wire mesh used to hold the plaster in place. Most of it was gone and lying in a pile on the floor. Billy wore a simple breathing mask and gloves. His job was threefold. First, pick out all the wooden lath, remove the nails, and pile it in the yard. Second, shovel the bits of plaster and wire into the wheelbarrow, and dump it on a tarp beside the truck. Finally, remove the nails from the bare studs in preparation for the new insulation and drywall. Billy was at the wheelbarrow stage. This was not his favorite job. Twice, he had over-filled the wheelbarrow and accidently dumped it as he wheeled it down the ramp. Getting the mess off the ground and back into the wheelbarrow seemed to take forever.

His dad was standing on the porch looking down at him shaking his head. "You know..." he began.

Billy interrupted, "...if you put less in the wheelbarrow it would take less time in the end. *I know.* I know."

"If you know, why do you insist on this?" His dad gestured at the pile of plaster on the front lawn.

"I had to figure out what was too much. The only way I could do that was to do this. Now I know. Okay!" replied Billy with an irritated tone.

His dad did not bother with an answer. He simply grinned, turned around, and walked back to the kitchen where he was working on mudding the new drywall. Billy dropped a large piece of plaster into the wheelbarrow and walked into the house. He watched his dad for a moment and then asked, "When is the guy from the university coming?"

His dad looked up at Billy. "Damn. I forgot. I have to go to town this afternoon. Can you let him into the cellar and show him the old forge? He said he was coming sometime this afternoon."

"Sure," said Billy. He turned around and continued his work.

After lunch, Billy continued to remove the mountain of

plaster and wire. As soon as his father left, he stopped and opened the trapdoor in the kitchen that led to the cellar. He climbed down the steps and pulled the string hanging from the newly-installed light bulb in the middle of the room. The room was brightly lit. Billy turned in circles, looking at the walls, forge, and shelf. He wondered if *this* forge had been used to meltdown stolen gold and pour it into the brass figurines. His eye caught a glint of yellow coming from one of the top cubbies on the back wall. He realized it was the head of the bright yellow screw he had used to secure the left panel. Now, even if you pulled on the hidden ring, the shelf would not open. He looked on the floor, reached down, and pinched some dirt between his fingers. He climbed up and wiped spit on the screw head, then rubbed the dirt over it, so it was invisible. He shut off the light hanging from the ceiling and unscrewed the bulb. He was pretty sure that Ed Upton would not find the hidden tunnel if he had to use a flashlight. All the brass ornaments he found on the shelf when he was cleaning were now in a box upstairs, waiting to be inspected by Mrs. Cooper. If he spent too much time inspecting the shelves, Billy would ask him if he wanted to see them and take him upstairs. He felt good about his plan.

Billy returned to his plaster cleanup and was nearly

finished when the white van from the university drove up and Ed Upton got out. He was followed by the girl.

"Hi, Billy," Upton said. He turned to the girl. "This is Ming. She works with me. Is your dad here?"

"Nope," said Billy. He no longer trusted Ed Upton after hearing their plans to search for hidden treasure—treasure that was Billy's to find.

"Will you show us the forge in the basement?" asked Ming in a sweet voice.

"There is no basement," said Billy bluntly. He stared at them suspiciously. "There is only a cellar. I'll show you. But you will need a flashlight. Lights don't work."

Ming opened the sliding door of the van and held up two flashlights. "We've come prepared."

Billy walked into the house and pointed at the kitchen floor and the open trapdoor. "It's down there." Ed and Ming climbed down the stairs, followed by Billy. "It is there. The forge. Don't step on that or the entire cellar will fill with dust."

Ming's flashlight swept to where Billy was pointing. "This is clearly a forge and that is the bellows." She turned to Ed. "Could someone use this to create brass ornaments?"

His flashlight swept over the forge. He did not pay any attention to the shelves on the back wall. Billy did not even look in that direction. He did not want to draw even the slightest bit of attention to it. Finally, Billy said, "I've got a bunch of the brass animals upstairs. You want to see them?"

Both Ed and Ming's faces brightened. In unison they said, "Sure! Very much."

Billy turned to the stairs and walked up, followed by the other two. He closed the trapdoor and headed into one of the bedrooms where he had put the box of ornaments. He pointed. "They are in there. You can have a look. I have to get back to work." He turned to go and then a perfect lie jumped into his head. He turned back and said, "We made an inventory of everything in the box and sent it to Mrs. Cooper. She is the owner." He figured they would not be able to get away with stealing anything from the box if they thought there was an inventory. "Take your time."

Billy had finished the plaster cleanup and started on the third part of the job, pulling an infinite number of nails from the studs. When they installed the lath, they seemed to think that if two nails were good then 50 nails were better. The heads of the nails were black and hard to see. Billy ran his hand along the stud to feel for any nails he had missed. One nail left behind could punch a hole in the new sheet-rock that his father would soon install. He was standing on a small step ladder, running his hand down the stud he had just completed when the two university students came out. They were carrying two small brass ornaments. They held them out in front of them. Billy turned as they exited and pulled his hand away from the stud. It caught on the sharp edge of a protruding nail he had missed and cut the palm of his hand. He jumped to the floor and cried out, "Ouch."

The girl moved toward him with concern in her voice. "Are you okay?"

Billy looked down at his hand. He was bleeding from a cut the nail had torn in his palm. He instinctively moved his hand to his mouth to suck the blood.

The girl took a step forward and grabbed his arm. "Don't put that in your mouth." Billy looked up at her questioningly. "Some of these old houses have mold and fungi spores that can make you very sick. These old houses tend to harbor them in the walls." She pointed at some old tar paper in the walls. "It can grow on that. You should have a breathing mask."

Billy looked at his mask that was sitting on a box in the corner of the room. "I thought it was for dust. Since I stopped making dust I took it off."

"It would be better to keep it on. One of my archeology

courses covered the dangers of finding old books and scrolls that contain ancient mold spores. They can make you very sick."

Ed Upton stepped forward. "Ming, you are scaring the kid." He turned to Billy. "The most common effect is a mild allergic reaction. Do you think we can borrow these? We will return them in perfect condition."

Billy pulled a painting rag from his back pocket and pressed it into his bleeding hand. "You will have to ask my dad. He should be back soon."

"Sounds good. We will wait on the stoop. You better wash that hand," said Ming.

They went out to wait for Billy's father to arrive. He drove in just as Billy turned on the hose and started to wash the wound on his hand.

TRANSLATIONS

CHAPTER 24

After dinner, Billy's dad asked to see his hand. After a brief inspection, he grunted, "Worse than I thought. You should have shown this to me sooner." He got out the first-aid kit and removed a bottle of disinfectant. "Hold your hand over the sink. This is going to sting a little, but if you leave it, an infection will set in and that will hurt a heck of a lot more." Billy winced as the disinfectant was poured over the jagged cut. His father cleaned the wound with a piece of gauze, put some ointment on it, and bandaged it up. "This will hurt some over the next few days. I am giving you tomorrow off. I want you to keep an eye on it for infection. If it starts to get red and more painful than it already is let me know. And this reminds me, we should take you into the walk-in clinic to get a new tetanus shot. It's been a few too many years."

Billy looked up at him. Needles were not his favorite

thing. "I'll keep it clean." His dad had given him a couple of safety lectures that explained what tetanus was. He would keep the wound clean. It was not very deep, and he felt sure that it would heal. Still, he decided to let his dad worry a little—if it got him a day off. Immediately, he felt a tinge of guilt for thinking about taking advantage of his dad's need to care for him. But he brushed it aside and started to make plans for his unexpected day off.

First, he would inspect the buckle and see if he could read the scratching. He took a candle, matches, and piece of aluminum foil to his room. He lit the candle and held the aluminum foil over the flame until the thin metal was covered in a fine soot. He extinguished the candle and blew on the foil until it was cool enough to touch. He smeared the soot on his index finger and rubbed it into the small scratches on the buckle. After a few minutes, he could see some shapes. They made absolutely no sense to him. He turned the buckle upside down in the hope that some meaning would jump out at him. Nothing did. He set the buckle down and then picked it up and spun it again on the end of a sharp pencil. He could clearly make out the image of the house, shed, and out crop on the median of the freeway. They were all joined with a wiggly line. "Well, Mr. Wong, your belt buckle clearly shows the tunnel, but what the heck are these other markings?" said Billy out loud. *Mr. Wong!* The owner of the buckle was *Chinese.* He peered again at the markings. They were saying something written in Chinese. Billy did not know anyone who could read Chinese. His old piano teacher was Chinese, but she had moved away last year. And anyway, if he asked someone to translate, he might have to explain about the buckle. That was his secret and, until he figured it out, it would remain his secret.

He started to draw what he saw on paper:

砖门键三

When he finished, he headed out to ask his dad if he could look something up on his computer. He stopped. His father would ask what he was looking up and he had to have a reasonable lie ready instead of the truth. He couldn't say, "I'm looking up some Chinese words I found on the belt buckle I never told you I found in Mr. Wong's grave that showed me the tunnel, that I also never told you about, that might lead to a treasure of gold, silver, and jewels." Suddenly, he knew he had the perfect lie. He remembered Ming talking about mold and how it could make you sick. That was what he was going to look up. Mold.

Billy stepped into the living room. His dad was doing what he usually did. He was watching the TV and reading a book at the same time. If he asked his dad why he did both at the same time the answer would be, "Because I hate to waste time. As soon as a commercial comes on or the show gets predictable I read my book. That way I am never bored." "May I use the computer in your office? I want to look something up."

His dad responded, "Sure," without looking up from his book. A truck commercial blared.

Billy knew he would get asked for details later, so he immediately looked up "dangers of mold" then clicked a new tab. He typed in, "translate Chinese characters into English" and hit enter. There were a lot of sites that would translate English into Chinese, but how would you translate Chinese into English? He scrolled down the screen and saw what he needed:

Find Chinese characters online by drawing them with your mouse.

He went to the page, unfolded the slip of paper he had drawn the Chinese characters and proceeded to draw them into a small box on the website. He chose the easiest character first. He drew three horizontal lines with the mouse. To the right of his drawing there was a grid of sixteen possibilities that changed as he drew. He clicked on the one that looked the most like his drawing. The word sān popped up. Billy clicked on translate. The site told him the word meant "three." He continued with the other characters and was rewarded with the following:

三 – Sān – three 门 – Mén – gate 砖 – Zhuān – block 键 – Jiàn – key

When the word "key" came up, Billy's heart rate jumped. He read the words over and over trying out different orders until the little rhyme filled his head: *gate key, block three.*

He repeated it over and over. The first part was obvious. The key fit the lock on the barred gate at the end of the tunnel. The second part was where the key was located: brick three. The wall that blocked the tunnel from the cellar was made of bricks, and bricks were just blocks after all. Maybe one of them concealed the key. But which one was the third block? Just then the TV volume dropped. Billy quickly clicked on the mold tab of the browser. His dad came in and Billy said, "Hey, Dad, did you know that you can get chronic lung disease from breathing in spores from old books. Ming told me that they can also be in old houses like the Cooper's and I should always wear my mask."

"That's why I got it for you," he grunted. "I'm going

upstairs to read. I will probably fall asleep, so I will say goodnight now. In the morning, I have to go across town to give a quote on a new job starting in October. We should be finished with the Cooper place by then. I will be gone most of the day. What are you up to on your day off?"

"Thought I would plan a sleepover tomorrow night in our hideout fort. Okay with you?"

"Have fun. Be safe," he said and turned towards his bedroom then disappeared.

"Night, Dad," Billy called after him. "I'm going to bed too." He shut down the browser and went to his room. He had to consider his next move. He had to find the key and open the lock. If he was able to do that, he would be one step closer to finding any treasure that might be hidden.

PLANS
TO
GO
IT
ALONE

CHAPTER 25

Billy slept in. Dreams of fame and riches filled is head. They seem to be exciting at the start, but all too soon became "complicated." That was the best word he could find to express the pattern of his dreams. The complicated part started when the dream story could not decide which path to take. It would follow a story line that filled with possibilities, too many possibilities, most of which were not pleasant. Once the dream became complicated, he would abandon it and start over. Lies and half-truths were usually the problem. He would find gold ingots and get his name in the paper. He would get interviewed on the TV news. He would get phone calls from Ellen and Oprah. If someone asked him a question that he had previously lied about, he would feel ill. If that happened in his dream, he would immediately start the dream over, hoping to avoid having his father and all his friends know he had lied to them. The only good part of his fantasy was solving the puzzle and finding treasure.

He wasn't so sure there was any treasure. After all, Ed Upton had said that the Chinese gang had been destroyed and no gold was found. Maybe that was because there was no gold to find. Maybe the Cooper place had nothing to do with the Chinese thieves. But then there was Mr. Wong, the murdered Chinese man buried right beside the entrance to the tunnel in the shed. There was the buckle with directions to something, and a clue to the location of the key. Then there was the tunnel with a barred-gate at the end.

Billy woke up. It was late morning. He got up and washed, ate breakfast, and got dressed. All of which he did while lost in thought. He pushed the tension of his dreams aside. He could not live with himself if he did not discover what was on the other side of the barred gate. To do that, he had to find a key or....An idea came to him. He was going to invite the gang for a sleepover. After all, it was Friday night. *But what if he didn't?* What if he slept in the fort by himself and used the darkness to cross the freeway. Crossing the freeway in daylight was almost impossible. Summer traffic was nonstop, and someone might see him. But before that, he would look for a key down in the tunnel. The barred gate was in the tunnel, so it only stood to reason that the key was hidden there, too. A plan was forming. He grabbed his LED flashlights and tested them, then stuffed the elastic headband that turned the flashlights into a geek light into his pocket and ran out the door.

He headed for the boulevard where the Braves usually met. Jackie would not be there. He was grounded for another seven days. He felt bad for Jackie. Two weeks was a fifth of the summer. He rounded the corner and saw Petra, Orph, Maddox, and Sharming tossing a frisbee back and forth. He was about to turn around. He wanted to avoid them. Sharming saw him and shouted, "William." Everyone looked, and he ran over to them.

"Hi, guys," he said.

"Spread out, you guys. Make room for Billy," said Maddox.

Petra came over to him. She had a big smile on her face. "Where you been, Billy? I missed you." She touched him on the shoulder.

Billy felt his face flush with embarrassment. He was not used to having girls like Petra telling the world she missed him. He quickly moved away to reach a place to catch the frisbee and shouted, "I had to work all week for my dad." The frisbee was tossed around the circle. Only Sharming had problems. Every time he tried to toss it, it hit the ground a meter in front of him. Orph went to show him and soon he was able to toss it as well as the rest of them. Billy's position was near the old maple. A toss from Maddox sailed over his head and he ran to catch it. The frisbee landed in the maple tree. The whole gang ran over. They all automatically scanned the boulevard for witnesses. Keeping the secret passage to the Cooper Property secret was ingrained in all of them. No one was in sight. Billy was about to climb the tree to fetch the frisbee when he heard voices from the other side of the eight-foot concrete fence. He stopped and held his finger up to shush the gang. They all listened. Billy immediately recognized Ed and Ming's voices. There was also the telltale hum of a metal detector.

Billy gestured the gang to come in closer and whispered, "It's the people from the university, checking out the yard again. I'm going to climb up and have a look. You guys stay here." He carefully climbed the tree and peeked through the leaves. He could see a much larger machine sitting in the middle of the yard. Attached to it were scanning wands with small iPad-like screens attached. Both Ming and Ed were systematically covering the entire Cooper property.

He heard Ming speak. She pointed at the screen on the top of her wand. "So, this is the graph that shows if there are any hollows areas underground that are different in density to the surrounding areas."

"Yeah. If something were buried up to two-meters deep you would see a variation on that graph."

"You mean, like another grave?"

"Yep. Or a cache of gold-filled brass animals."

"That is a fantasy. There is no treasure buried next to the freeway."

"Probably not. But let me know if you notice an underground hollow. I looked up the geology of this area. On the far side of the Cornbourgh Estates the excavation crew found a cave system. They are all filled in now." Billy froze. They might find his tunnel. If he was going to solve the mystery before they did he would have to act. He would have to act *tonight*.

"I have a seminar to lead this afternoon. You know what Prof Halverson will do if he walks into my seminar and I am fumbling. I can fool the first years but not him. Let's go. You can scan along the fence and behind the shed tomorrow. It's Saturday, and he gave you permission to scan it all."

"Yeah, okay. It's just that I was hoping to get it all done today."

"It's not going anywhere. You can look for your lost treasure tomorrow." She disconnected her scanning wand and headed to the white university van. Ed reluctantly followed, wheeling the scanning device. They loaded the van and drove away. Billy shook a branch and the frisbee dropped to the ground. He soon followed.

"Well, that ends my plans. I was planning to ask you guys if you wanted to have another sleepover in the fort, but the guys from the university will be here tomorrow."

"Maybe we can sleepover Saturday night," said Orph.

"I cannot," said Sharming. "I have to attend my cousin's wedding. I am the bearer of the rings."

"Yeech," said Maddox.

"The food is plentiful and very, very good," said Sharming.

"Well," said Billy, "maybe next Friday. Everyone keep the date open if you can." They all nodded.

SEARCHING
FOR
THE
KEY

Billy headed home and packed his sleeping bag and other necessary camping gear into his knapsack. He wrote a note to his dad saying he would be home sometime on Saturday afternoon. Then he waited. It was critical that he did not meet any of his friends on his way to the maple tree. It was also important that he left before his dad came home. It was too soon to leave, so he waited and planned what he needed to do.

After an hour, he figured that all his friends would have gone home, so he headed out. Avoiding the straight route, he stuck to the alleys behind the houses. Also, by moving from cover to cover, he avoided the streets that any of his friends lived on. Tucked behind a large mailbox unit, scanning the street, he hoped it would be empty. He saw no one. Unfortunately, he stepped out just as Mr. Kirk came out of his front door. He was walking straight toward

Billy. His stride was purposeful, and Billy thought he was staring straight at him. In fact, he was, but only because Billy was standing right in front of the mailbox. Mr. Kirk was carrying a mail key in his hand. Billy lowered his head and strode forward. Just as he passed Billy, Mr. Kirk said, "Hello, William."

"Hello, Mr. Kirk," said Billy without stopping.

They passed each other and then Mr. Kirk turned and called back to Billy. "Oh, William, I meant to call you about doing a little yard work." Billy had worked for Mr. Kirk before, mowing lawns and such.

"Any time, Mr. Kirk, just give me a call. Got to go right now. Sorry," said Billy and he rushed off down the last alley before the boulevard. He looked both ways. Seeing no one, he rushed across to the maple tree. With one last look, he climbed the tree, crossed the branch, and dropped down on the shed roof.

Billy had already decided that he was not going to sleep up in the tree fort. He was going to sleep in the shed. He did not want to be climbing to the fort in the dark. He went in the shed and removed his pack. While it was still light, he had to go into the house and get some bulbs to replace the one that had burned out. He would also get a spare. He retrieved the key to the back door and went inside. After finding the bulbs and setting them by the door, he picked up his dad's screw gun, removed the battery from the charger, and snapped it in. He tested the gun. It spun reassuringly in his hand. He lifted the trapdoor to the cellar and descended the ladder. After tightening the bulb, he pulled the dangling string, and the room filled with stark light. He pushed a box over to the shelf and removed the screw he had previously put into the shelf. He placed the screw gun in one of the cubbies on the shelf that did not move, then reached up and pulled the ring in the top cubby. The opposite shelf swung open. The air was still dank and musty, but the spiders hadn't had time to rebuild their webs. He pointed his flashlight into the cave and jumped down.

Billy went straight down the tunnel. The Chinese lettering said "block" and "three," so Billy figured he would look here. *Bricks were blocks, right?* The wall was made of bricks, so maybe one of them held the key—or at least *a clue* to where the key might be. He sat down in front of the brick wall that blocked off the tunnel, scanning the bricks with his flashlight beam as he counted and tapped and listened and rubbed and pushed and pulled on any brick that could possibly be the third one, depending on how you counted. There was no key. He stood up and bumped his head on a slight protrusion in the ceiling. He turned while rubbing his head, climbed up onto the shelf, and pushed the shelf closed. He grabbed the screw gun and was about to replace the screw when he realized it was no longer necessary, so he jumped down with gun in hand. He turned to go up the ladder when he had another thought, *Cubbies were blocks—sort of, anyway. Maybe the key was hidden in one of them, and I missed it when I cleaned up.* Billy searched the cubbies, one by one, rubbing his hand over all the surfaces. There was nothing.

Billy had another idea. Maybe he had put the key in the box that was to go to Mrs. Cooper. Maybe it didn't look like a key. Maybe he had already found it and hadn't even noticed. Maybe it was in the box upstairs. He quickly shut off the light, climbed the stairs into the kitchen, and closed the trapdoor. He went into the bedroom where he had put the box and searched through everything. There was nothing that looked like a key. He closed the box, replaced the screw gun, and put the battery back on the charger. He grabbed the two bulbs beside the door and locked up. A few minutes later, he was heading back to the shed. The sky had turned grey. It was heavy with clouds. Billy knew these clouds meant rain. He really hoped it would hold off. He didn't want his dad to get worried and come out looking for him.

Once in the shed, Billy continued with the search for the elusive key. He plugged in the cord that powered his light string. He opened the trapdoor in the shed floor and lowered the ladder. He descended, put his geek light on, and headed up the tunnel toward the house. He was not going to leave any "brick" unturned, as it were. He soon came to a stop in front of the other side of the brick wall. He went straight to the pile of leftover bricks that were strewn on the ground. He looked each one over carefully but found nothing. He inspected the brick wall from this side with the same intensity as he had in the cellar. There was nothing.

Billy walked back down the tunnel, picked up the replacement bulb, and continued down the tunnel. It was brightly lit by his string of bulbs until he came to the burned out one. He quickly replaced it and continued to the end. He was once again at the barred gate. He tried to reach through the bars to inspect the lock in the light of a 100-watt bulb. He could just touch it with his fingers. There was no way to even smash the lock from this side. He could see beyond the gate. There was what appeared to be a small cave. The ceiling was wet and dripping water from some newly-formed stalagmites. He took out his flashlight and pointed the beam into the dark where the bulb behind him did not illuminate. There were a number of small pockets along the floor of the cave. Beyond that was, what appeared to be, another smaller cave. He could see no further. If he wanted to search on the other side of the barred gate he would have to cross the freeway, find an entrance, and climb inside. He considered the problem. There were a number of "what-ifs." *What if he could not find a way into the cave? What if there was no entrance?* It could be totally blocked up. Billy did not want to consider that possibility. He suddenly came to the conclusion that the key must be on the other side of the gate, simply because the lock was on the other side of the gate. There would be no point in hiding a key on this side if you could not use it to open the lock. If it was anywhere, it had to be in that cave on the other side of the bars. He pointed his flashlight through the bars and scanned the cave again. He stopped on one of the small cave-like indentations near the floor. There was something inside. He leaned closer to the bars until his face was pressed against them in an effort to make out what was in this small hole in the wall. He noticed a right-angled shadow. His pulse fluttered. It might be a brick. It might hold the key.

He shut off his flashlight, and tucked it in his pocket

just as a thunder clap rolled overhead. The vibration reached right down into the tunnel with an amplified bang. There was another larger rumble and suddenly the lights went out. Billy was standing in total darkness. He realized that the dark clouds he had noticed earlier were now thunderheads. He turned toward a flash of light in the direction of the barred gate when another thunder clap pounded down the tunnel. The lightening that preceded the thunder had lit up the darkness.

Once again, the light flashed at the back of the cave on the far side of the gate, followed almost immediately by the thunder. Billy knew at once that there must be an entrance. The light from the lightning flash was evidence there was a hole. The size of the hole was still unknown, but it must be large enough to allow that much light into the cave. Chills ran up his spine and down his arms. He just had to check it out. He searched for his flashlight and turned it on just as the light string came back on. He ran down the tunnel. He did not want to be caught in the darkness again.

CAPTURED

The string of lights flickered a couple of times before he reached the tunnel section under the shed. Once there, they went out completely. There was a power failure. Billy climbed up the ladder and pulled it up after him. He closed the trapdoor and sat down on his rolled sleeping bag. It wasn't late enough to try to cross the freeway. There were still too many cars. His head filled with fantasies of finding treasure, each one interrupted by reality. He had kept all this tunnel and treasure stuff secret from everyone, even his best friend and his dad. Was he being driven mad by his desire to find treasure? Did he have "gold fever?" He had learned about that in school when they did a unit on the gold rush in Social Studies. Maybe he had it? People with gold fever did crazy things for gold. *Was he doing crazy things?* What if he *did* find gold at the other end of the tunnel? What then? Would he tell everyone? If he did, they might take it all away from him. He might get his name in the paper, but he wouldn't get any gold. The government would take it.

Billy lay back on the floor with his sleeping bag under his head. He stared at the ceiling. "I'm just a kid," he said out loud. He then thought, *If I wasn't a kid, I might be able to take the gold, hide it, and find a place to melt it down into small ingots and sell them whenever I needed money.*

He suddenly sat up. He had a plan. He was going to hide any gold that he found and leave it there until he was old enough to melt it down and sell it. Then it wouldn't matter if he told everyone about the tunnel. He just needed to leave out the part about the gold. *But where would he hide it?* Ed Upton and Ming were bound to find the tunnel using the metal/density scanner. If there was gold on the other side of the barred gate, he would have to find it and move it as soon as possible.

Billy jumped to his feet. He checked his pockets for things he might need. He had a flashlight, the felt pen he used to mark the studs when he had removed all the nails, and his small jackknife. He clipped the rock-hammer to his belt and stepped out of the shed. It was dark. The power was out all over the Glen. He walked toward the freeway. There was light over in the Cornbourgh Estates on the other side of the freeway. A power transformer probably blew out or was hit by lightning, killing the power on this side of the freeway. He looked skyward and could see some sheet lightning in the distance. The storm was heading west. He looked down at the freeway. There were cars on the other side but nothing on his side. He trudged through the brush until he reached the edge of the road. He saw headlights approaching. He crouched down. A car passed. Darkness closed in. Billy took out a flashlight from his pouch and sprinted across the road, up an incline of loose rocks, and into the light brush on the other side.

He stopped and was breathing hard—not from the run but from the excitement and fear he felt. All he needed to do now was to find the entrance to the tunnel. He headed for the rock tower in the middle of the median. He concealed himself in the trees and walked uphill to the north. His flashlight scanned the ground. Some large boulders came into view. Billy walked around them. He knew the light from the lightning bolt had entered the cave from somewhere, somewhere very close to here.

There was a pile of smaller rocks and then the beginning of the rock tower. Billy searched around the base of the tower. At the east-most point, the ground fell away. It was a pit with rocks all around the edge and fiddlehead ferns growing in the middle of it. Billy pointed his light down into the pit and jumped in. He found a small opening in the side of the pit about a half meter round. He crouched down and pointed his light into the hole. He heart was pounding in his chest. "This is it," he thought. All he could see was more darkness. He stuck his head in the hole and started to crawl down the passage way. He had gone about a meter when the passage opened up into a larger cavern. Billy scanned the cavern with his flashlight. His entire body shivered, and the goose bumps ran up and down his spine. Right in front of him was the gate of metal bars, and dangling from the gate was the biggest and oldest padlock Billy had ever seen. He was here. Now all he had to do was find the key to the lock.

"Gate – Key, Block –Three" … rang out in his mind. He inspected the cavern, starting in the small rectangular alcoves on one side where the cave wall met the floor. There were some bricks in the first one. They were the same kind of bricks that had been used to wall up the tunnel leading to the forge. He moved quickly to the bricks. There was a pile three bricks wide and three bricks high. The bricks touching the floor were almost disintegrated with water and age. The ones on top were still intact. Billy picked them up one at a time and inspected them. They were just

old, red, clay bricks. Leftovers. *Which one was brick three?* he thought. He dug into the shards of the bottom three bricks but found nothing. He tapped the others with his rock hammer and each gave a resounding thunk. He hit one of the bricks hard with the rock hammer. A large crack formed at an angle. He hit it again and it broke into two pieces. He held them up and inspected the broken faces. Nothing looked like a key. He sat back and ran his flashlight around the base of the cavern. He counted four rectangular openings at the base. The one that held the bricks was the largest, measuring about 40-centimeters square. The other three were increasingly smaller. Billy pointed his light at each in turn. The smallest one was about the size of one of the bricks. In fact, one brick would fit right inside of it. None of them were very deep. Billy crouched down and looked into the second hole. It was shallow and empty. He slid over to the third hole that appeared to be deeper. He was about to reach inside when he heard the sound of a police siren gradually getting closer and closer. He froze, expecting the siren to pass by and disappear into the distance. It did not. It was suddenly very loud and very near.

Billy pointed his flashlight into the hole he had used to enter the cavern. His first thought was that his dad had come to rescue him from the storm. He probably talked to one or more members of the gang and discovered the location of the fort. He would be wondering why he had gone to the fort by himself. Maybe he even called the cops. What if these were real cops looking for him? He crawled out of the tunnel, out of the hole, around the large boulders to the bushes three meters from the edge of the freeway. He tucked his LED flashlight into his pocket. Standing on the top of a slope of loose gravel, he could see the police car and in front of it was a semi-truck with the name of a large electronics store chain on the side. The realization that these were the hijackers at work again made Billy freeze. This section of the freeway was the only place there was room for a semi to pull over on the left. The hijackers could conceal themselves between the treed median on the left and the truck on the right. His skin was growing cold.

He watched through the thick brush as one of the men wearing a police uniform walked up the driver's side of the truck to the cab. Billy could not see clearly, but it appeared as if the policeman had ordered the driver to open the cab door. The fake cop climbed up to the cab, swung something at the driver, and climbed into the driver seat. Billy realized there were two other men in the police car. Both wore dark coveralls and black toques. Billy watched as one of them got out and ran up the side of the truck. When he reached the cab, the fake policeman climbed down. Billy could just make out their conversation.

"Is he out?" asked the man wearing the toque.

"Yeah. I hit him pretty hard. You can dump him. He won't be talking anytime soon. I injected him with this," he said and held up a needle that he slipped into a case.

"He saw your face. Are you sure we shouldn't make perfectly sure?"

"I tell you he won't remember a thing. Just dump him in the usual place and put this package in his pocket."

"What is it?"

"Insurance money and a little note. He will wake up and not remember what happened to his truck, but he has a thousand dollars in his pocket that he cannot account for and a note that recommends he don't even try to remember. Even if he tells the cops, it's doubtful they will ever connect it to us."

"Okay. Hope you know what you're doing."

"Just drive the truck to the warehouse and then dump the driver. That cannot be too difficult."

The hijacker nodded, climbed into the truck cab, and drove away. The fake cop walked back to the cop car. The other man was leaning on the hood of the car with his toque in his hands. "Let's go. There's another truck due soon. We have to get ourselves set. There is a turnaround just past the curve. We can head north again. About four klicks further, there is another turnaround. We will wait there until the truck passes, follow him, and pull him over right here."

"Sounds good. This is a perfect spot. No one can see anything from over there," he said, gesturing in the direction of the Glen.

The fake cop opened the car door and the other man slipped his toque on his head and walked to the passenger side. Billy leaned forward, trying to see inside the car. He wanted to know if it looked like a cop car inside as well as out. The loose gravel slipped out from under his feet. He fell on his bum and slid down the hill. He stopped practically at the fake cop's feet. He tried to get up, but the rocks moved under his feet, and he could not hold his footing. He turned over, pushed himself to a standing position, and started to scramble up the slope. He got half a step when he was lifted from the ground by the scruff of his neck.

"What do we have here?" Billy was turned around in the air. He tried to get loose, kicking out with his feet and swinging his arms. The fake cop reached out with his other hand and slapped Billy hard across the face. "A little spy."

He turned to the other man. "Get the duct tape from the backseat."

"Let me go! Let me go!" screamed Billy. The man hit him hard again on the side of his face. Billy felt his face stinging from the slap. He wanted to cry but decided he would not give these criminals the satisfaction. The fake cop slammed Billy down on the trunk of the car and held him while the other man taped his hands and legs. A final piece of tape was wrapped tautly around his head, covering his mouth. Billy moaned.

The cop inspected his work. "What the hell are you doing out here at this time of night anyway?" Billy moaned again. "Oh, that's right, you have tape over your mouth," he said and laughed.

They opened the trunk of the car, dumped him inside, and covered him with an old smelly blanket. The trunk slammed closed and the darkness was total, except for the bursts of light behind Billy's eyes that swelled and ebbed with the pain in his face.

escapeD

The car started to move. The trunk vibrated as the car accelerated. Billy gagged at the smell of the old blanket covering him. He forced himself to breathe slowly. His heart rate slowed, and he took stock of his situation. His hands were crossed over each other and wrapped with duct tape. All he could move was the index finger of his right hand. He lifted his arm to his face and started to wiggle his one movable finger under the tape that was over his mouth. Soon he was able to draw air through his mouth. His sense of being suffocated ebbed. He knew he had to get his hands free first. He lifted his knees up to his chest and then straightened his legs out. His runners caught on the blanket and pulled it off his head. The air was suddenly cooler, and Billy sucked it in greedily through the small opening under the tape. He reached his hands up and felt the trunk lid hoping to find something sharp to cut the tape. If he could get his hands free he might be able to escape. If he didn't, he would be at the mercy of these men and he suspected they had no mercy for anyone, especially a witness to their crime, but he found nothing. Billy kicked his feet up at the trunk lid. They hit with a resounding thud.

"Stop thumping around in there, kid, or I will wrap you up like a mummy," shouted the voice of the fake cop.

Billy stopped. He pushed out of his mind the panic that was threatening to overwhelm him and bring tears to his eyes. He knew he had a small jackknife in his back pocket, but there was no way to reach it. He brought his knees up to his chest and reached down with his taped-up hands. He felt the tape around his ankles. Most of it was sticking to his hi-top running shoes and the top of his jeans. He wiggled his feet in the hope he could get his feet free. He was not sure that would help him, but it was a start. An idea jumped into his mind and he started to use the one free finger to undo the snap on his jeans. He released it after some effort. The zipper was easier, and slowly it opened. Billy was going to take his pants off and with them would come his shoes. He could then get at the jackknife he always carried in his back pocket. Billy was very conscious of noise. He did not want to give the men any reason to stop and check on what he was doing.

He wiggled and wormed and undulated his body until he was able to pull his legs out of his shoes and jeans. He was breathing hard. The sweat was dripping down his face. He had also freed almost all of the fingers of his right hand. His thumb was another matter. It was still firmly locked beneath the tape.

Once his pants were off, he searched for the knife. He felt it through his jeans, along with a black sharpie. He got the knife out of his jeans back pocket, worked the blade up, and began to cut away the tape holding his hands. Suddenly, they were free. He pulled off the remaining tape from his hands and mouth. A cell phone chimed. He froze and listened.

"Yeah," said the man with the toque. "Okay. We are heading north. Let us know when the truck passes you and we will cross over and come up behind it. Okay."

"How long?" asked the fake cop.

"Ten or fifteen," answered the other.

Billy picked the tape off his shoes and pants. He wiggled back into his pants and felt for his flashlight, found it, and pulled it out. He turned it on, found his knife, and returned it to his pocket. He swept the inside of the trunk. The blanket was in the way, so he yanked on it. It was caught on something. He yanked harder and it suddenly came free with a click. Billy's hand slammed back into the side of the trunk with a loud thump.

"Listen kid, one more sound out of you and you will think that little slap I gave you was just a love tap," the fake cop yelled and chuckled. "In a way, it was, 'cause I loved doing it. I will love to punch you in the face even more. I will love to see that itty bitty nose of yours crushed under my large knuckles."

Billy heard both men laugh. He stopped moving. He was breathing hard and concentrating on slowing it down. He did not want to be punched in the face.

Billy lay quiet. He could feel a cool breeze coming into the trunk from somewhere. He twisted his body until he was facing the trunk latch. He pointed his flashlight at it. It seemed to be moving up and down. Billy reached out and touched the trunk just above the latch. He felt the entire trunk start to swing open. Surprised, he grabbed it and pulled it back down. He remembered the "click" when he yanked on the smelly blanket. It must have been caught in the latch of the trunk. When he pulled it out, the latch released, and the trunk unlocked. He now had a way out of the trunk when the car stopped. *If the car stopped.*

Billy remembered the lesson his dad taught him when

he got his first skateboard. It had something to do with relativity and inertia. He could not remember how those words fit into the explanation, but he did remember what happened when he first stepped off of a moving skateboard. It felt like someone had grabbed both his feet and pulled them out from underneath him. He landed flat on his face. But that was when he was eight. He figured jumping out of a moving car would be a heck of a lot worse. He had to wait until the car stopped before he tried to escape. And he had to peek just before he jumped out, so he knew where he was going to run. Jumping out would be a waste of time if he was captured again before he was able to go anywhere.

The air rushing past the edges of the unlatched trunk was noisy, but not noisy enough to cover the whispers he could hear from the two men in the car.

"Have you decided what we are going to do with our bundle in the trunk?" asked the man in the coveralls. Billy pulled down on the trunk to reduce the air noise that whistled in his ears. "We can't let him go."

"I know," said the fake cop. "I'm thinking. After this truck, we will do something."

"What?"

"We'll have to head north again. I know this little lake.

It has a couple of cabins, but no one is staying in them. I figure we have to make it look like an accident. We'll remove the tape and bang his head on the side of a rowboat. Then we'll take one of the other boats and drag him out to the middle of the lake, dump him into the water, release the rowboat, and paddle back to shore. It will look like he stole a boat to go for a paddle, fell overboard, bashed his head, and drowned."

Billy felt sick. They were talking about murdering him. Billy reached into his back pocket and took out the sharpie. He was about to write something on the under lid of the trunk when he heard the man in the overalls speak. "That lake is at least 10-k off the highway. How the heck is a kid like that going to get there, and why would he paddle out into the lake just to fall overboard? It all sounds pretty suspicious to me and I am not even a cop."

"It will be a mystery." Billy could practically hear the fake cop grin. "A mystery that will never be connected to us."

"Whatever. Sounds good."

Billy stuck his flashlight in his mouth and started to write. "HIJACKERS—FAKE COPS—KILLED—WILLIAM BRAITHWAITE —250-555-2143—DROWNED ME IN A LAKE" He whispered to himself, "The cops will never see this. Shit." He lay back and breathed slowly. Suddenly, he sat up and nearly bashed his head. Rolling over to the trunk latch, he opened the trunk just enough to slip his hand out. He reached down and traced the letters and numbers of the license plate of the car. As each was revealed he repeated it in his head. He closed the trunk, rolled over on his back, pulled up his shirt and wrote on his chest: I WAS MURDERED—TGD 3UE—LOOK IN TRUNK—HIJACKERS. He pulled his shirt down again. At least now his body held clues to what they did to him and would maybe lead to their capture.

Billy laid back. He was caught between acceptance of his fate and the need to find a way out of this predicament. He heard a cell phone ring and the fake cop answered it.

"Yeah," said the cop. "Great." The car began to slow. Billy tensed his muscles in case he got an opportunity to jump out and run. The car stopped, and Billy sat up, pressing his hand to the top of the trunk. It opened slightly. Billy was about to slip out when lights hit him—lights from oncoming traffic. He felt a whoosh of diesel-laden air as a semi sped past. At the same time, the car started after the truck. Billy was flung back onto the trunk floor with a thump.

"Stay back. There is no need to be close until it's time to

pull him over," said one of the men.

"Yeah, okay. I'll turn on the lights when he approaches the curve. He will have to pull to the inside of the highway 'cause there is no room on the other side to park his rig. If he doesn't slow I will turn on the siren and force him over."

Billy waited and listened. He felt the car slow. He lifted the trunk lid slightly and saw the blue and red flashes of light coming from the ghost car driven by the hijackers. They had doubled-back to the median where they'd thrown him in the trunk. The car stopped, and he heard one door open. He reran their procedure over in his head. First, the fake cop gets out and approaches the driver whose door is facing the median, concealing him and the cop from any observers. The cop then hits the driver and injects him with something. He returns to the cop car and signals the man in the coveralls to drive the truck. Billy figured that the best time to go will be when both of the hijackers are at the truck. Billy counts silently, starting when he heard the second car door open. He got to thirteen and he opened the trunk just enough to slip out. He crouched down on the wet pavement. He peeked around the end of the car and saw the man in the coveralls climb up into the cab of the semi. The fake cop had his back to him. He was about to run when he realized he did not have any shoes on. He opened the trunk and reached in to grab them. He found them both and slipped one on. He was about to put the other shoe on when he felt a slight gust of wind. The trunk lid swung all the way open with a thump.

"What the hell!" shouted the fake cop from beside the rear of the semi-trailer. Billy started to run in a hop skip and jump fashion, carrying one shoe. He reached the edge of the median and turned to run up the rocky grade that led to the cave opening. He could hear a mixture of sounds— the truck engine starting up, the footsteps of the hijacker chasing him, and his own breath rushing in and out of his lungs. His one shoe-less foot stomped down on a sharp rock. He winced and hopped over the remaining gravel.

"You are going to pay for making me chase you. And I mean pay!" shouted the fake cop. The voice behind him was gaining. Billy turned and headed to the cave entrance. He needed to hide, and the only place he could think of was the cave. Suddenly, the ground dropped beneath his feet. He was falling into a depression filled with ferns. His bare foot screamed with pain. Billy knew he had cut it on the sharp rocks. He slipped the shoe he was carrying onto his wounded foot. The pain eased. The shoe acted like a bandage. He wiggled into the cave entrance. Breathing hard, he feared the man would hear him. He gradually slowed his ragged breathing and looked behind him. The power had come back on and he could see light. His string of lights was shining behind him, throwing a shadow to the cave opening! The fake cop might see the light and would catch him for sure if he didn't do something. He pulled some of the undergrowth from the depression into the cave opening and sat with his back to it in an effort to block all light from escaping, then waited and listened.

He could hear the occasional footstep and breaking branch as his pursuer searched for him in the darkness. A voice, suddenly very close, shouted. It was just at the lip of the depression. Billy suspected that the man was standing and looking down into the hole but could see nothing of the cave entrance.

"Hey, kid. I'll find out where you live." There was a pause, and then a little further away, the man continued, "I'll bet you live in Cornbourgh or the Glen. There will be no hiding from me if you breathe a word of this to anyone. I will find you, and when I do, I will kill you and everyone in your family. I will shoot your mother in the head. I will smash your dad's face in. I will save you for last, and you don't want to know what I will do to you." He laughed. "Bang, bang—smash, smash—stab, stab." There was no sound for a while. The man was listening and waiting for Billy to move. Billy didn't move a muscle. Billy was waiting for the sound of the car. There was only silence.

He waited. The only thing he moved was his eyes. His looked around the cave. His eyes stopped on the gate and the padlock. They drifted to the pile of bricks he had inspected earlier. It shifted to the other rectangular holes. Why were those holes cut so that they were almost perfect rectangles in the bottom of the cave wall? His eyes scanned each. They all seemed empty. He could see the light hit the back of all of them, except hole three.

Gate – Key, Block –Three

Maybe the block was not referring to a brick but a block-shaped hole. Still not daring to move because he knew the fake cop was waiting for him to reveal himself, he could only stare and imagine what the third hole in the wall might hold.

At least 10 minutes passed. Billy felt his legs beginning to cramp and his foot ache. Then he heard it. The car started. Some gravel crunched beneath its wheels and it pulled away from the shoulder. Billy shifted to a slightly more comfortable position, but he still waited. It might be a ploy to get him to come out of his hiding place. He listened but could hear nothing. He moved some of the brush away from the cave entrance and stuck his head out and listened. He heard a vehicle come down the freeway and drive right past without slowing down. He listened. Then he heard a footstep slip on the loose gravel that covered the incline. The fake cop was back. He must have driven down the road and then doubled back on foot. Billy carefully pulled the brush back into the hole and waited.

Billy heard the man mumble, "I guess he hightailed it. He didn't come out this side, so I bet he headed across the median to Cornbourgh. That cuts my search in half. I will be seeing him soon. He can bet on it." Billy heard him stomp across the loose gravel, then a car door slammed in the distance. The subsequent silence was broken only by the occasional passing car.

BACK TO SAFETY

Billy was tempted to go out and make sure the fake cop was truly gone but decided against it. The hijacker thought he was from Cornbourgh. He needed to keep it that way. He reached out of the cave opening and dragged even more brush into the hole. He knew he would have to go out the cave entrance if he was unable to find the key to the padlock. If he had to, he would wait for daylight. It would not be a good idea to fall again and he was still not positive the hijacker had really left. He turned his attention to the third rectangular hole. This one seemed deeper than the others. He could not see into the shadows deeper than the small beam coming from the light string could penetrate. He felt for his flashlight. It was no longer in his pocket. He must have dropped it in the trunk of the car. He slid across the cave floor and reached into the third hole. It was much deeper than he had expected and seemed to expand the further he reached. He was just able to reach the back with his fingers and arm fully extended. Sliding his hand from the back to the front, he felt the side walls and ceiling. His right hand was able to feel the left side. He turned onto his left shoulder and extended his left arm into the hole and continued to feel. On his second pass from back to front, his fingers touched something. It was half embedded in the wall of the hole. He grabbed it and pulled it out. It was a small, very heavy box, slightly smaller than a pencil box. His heart pounded. This was the key. He was sure of it. He tried to open the box, but it was corroded shut. Billy looked over at the bricks he had searched earlier and saw what he wanted. The rock hammer was lying on the ground where he had dropped it. He gently tapped the box on all sides with the hammer and finally it popped open. Billy stared at the contents. There were four small, flat black rectangles that lay like chocolates. Each one had a marking in the center. It was a Chinese symbol that resembled a house.

Billy hooked his nail under one of the little bricks that measured about five centimeters by three centimeters. It came out easily for it was about one-half centimeter thick.

There was another one underneath. He turned it in his hand. It had heft. Billy tossed it up and down to get a sense of its weight. He turned the whole box upside down and watched the little black bricks fall out. There were twelve in all: a dozen heavy little black bricks with a small house stamped into each. Billy started to place each of the bricks back into the box. One of them had fallen further away and struck the rock hammer when it fell. Billy picked it up and saw a glint of yellow on one corner. He scraped at the area with his fingernail. Some black, tar-like material came off under his nail. He stared at the golden color where he had scraped, and a realization flooded him. These were little bars of gold. He had found the gold treasure—or at least the part that had been left behind. He placed the small bars back into the box. With each bar came a shiver of excitement. He set the box down and continued to search the hole for other boxes. He did not find any. This one must have been missed because it had been embedded in the clay that lined the hole.

Billy sat with the box of gold in his lap. He started to fantasize about the gold. Suddenly, he shook his head, as if to shake away the daydreams he was falling into. He still had to get out of this cave. The best-case scenario would be to find the key, open the barred door, lock it again behind him and head back to the shed. The other option was not one he wanted. He was still afraid the hijacker was waiting for him if he had to cross the freeway. He went back to the holes in the walls. He felt inside all of them in turn. The very last one was small and shallow. He felt inside it with his fingers tracing any ridges and indentations. The back of the hole was hard—too hard for the clay that lined the other holes. He reached for his hammer and tapped the back of the small brick-sized hole. It was harder, emitting a thunk at each tap. Out of curiosity, Billy picked up one of the clay bricks that he had inspected earlier and tapped it with his hammer. It sounded exactly the same as the back of the small hole. He swung his hammer hard at the side walls and corner of the small hole and discovered the back wall was a brick. He pulled it out and felt behind it. There was nothing. He tapped the brick again and listened. He tapped one of the other bricks and listened. The one from the hole sounded hollow compared to the others. Billy set it down, lifted the hammer, and smashed the hollow-sounding brick dead center. Nothing happened. He picked it up, shook it and pulled at it. Suddenly, something gave way, and he was sitting with half a brick in each hand. The brick halves fit neatly together and had come apart. An old brass key lay sitting in his lap. He had found it.

Billy quickly got to his feet and crouched over the lock on the gate. The key fit perfectly into the lock. He tried to turn it, but it would not budge. He tapped the lock with his hammer and tried to turn the key at the same time. Gradually, it came free and the lock clicked. Billy pulled on the base and the shackle slowly cleared. He turned it to one side and lifted it from the hasp. He pulled on the gate. The hinges protested, screeching with each movement. Billy froze at the thought that he might be heard by the hijacker waiting above. He decided that he must be ready to open the gate, slam it shut behind him, and snap on the padlock. He picked up the box of what he now referred to as his chest of black gold, the hammer, key and the padlock. He slipped them all through the gate. He re-piled the bricks and put the key brick back in its place in the small hole. He inspected the floor. It was covered with his footprints. Grabbing a small fern that was sticking out of the cave entrance, he used it to sweep all traces of his trespass from the floor, then scanned his work for indications that someone had been in the cave recently. Feeling satisfied that anyone who found this cave would think they were the first in a very long time, he swept the floor beneath his feet with the fern, erasing the remaining footprints. He pulled open the gate that gave one short, loud squeal, stepped through, and closed it again to another squeal. He attached the lock and snapped it closed after freeing up the inside works by twisting and turning the shackle. The floor on the shed side of the gate was rock and left no trace of anyone passing. He picked up the box of gold, slipped the hammer into his belt, put the key in his pocket next to his knife, and picked up the end of the string of lights. He unscrewed the last bulb in the line a half turn to extinguish it, coiled the cord over his shoulder, and proceeded down the tunnel toward the shed. As he came to the next lit bulb, he did the same until he reached the ladder under the shed.

Billy had never been happier to see the ladder. It was like a pathway out of hell. It beckoned him, each rung more attractive than the previous. He proceeded to erase all trace that he had been down the tunnel. He removed the cords, ladder, and rope, and closed the trapdoor on the shed for the last time.

He had no idea what time it was, just sometime in the middle of the night. He looked himself over. He was sweaty and dirty and sore. It seemed like everything was hurting. He would go home and sneak into the house. His dad slept like death. Billy shook his head. He did not want to think of death. *His dad slept so deeply you could not wake him up unless you jumped on him.* That thought made Billy smile. He had often jumped on his sleeping dad when he was little. That almost always ended up in a wrestling match where his dad would tickle him until he cried "uncle."

He would sneak in, clean himself up, and crawl into bed. When his dad asked him about camping, he would say that the storm had scared all the gang, so he cancelled the sleep out and sent them home. In a week the lie would look like the truth. Billy decided he would have to think seriously about not telling any more lies.

The hijackers would not come up. He would not tell a soul.

As for the gold—well, that would be his secret, and it might come in handy sometime down the road.

NEARLY
ALL
IS
EXPOSED

Billy slipped into the house, cleaned up his hands, face and foot. It was bleeding a little, so he wrapped it in toilet paper and went to bed. His dreams were filled with multi-headed monsters that threatened to kill him and all his family if he did not do their bidding.

He woke to his father throwing clothes at him.

"Get up, Billy. I figured you might give up on the sleepover after the storm started." Billy moaned. "Get up. It's Saturday—laundry day. Bring all your dirty clothes out PDQ." Billy groaned again. "Alright, you can sleep a little longer. You worked really hard this week." His father started to pick up all his clothes. He looked at Billy half covered with blankets. "Take off that t-shirt. It's filthy." He reached down and pulled a half-sleeping Billy to a sitting position and pulled his t-shirt up and over his head.

Billy flopped back down on his back and moaned, "Let me sleep just a little longer."

Billy could feel his dad staring down at him. Suddenly, Billy was awake with the realization that his father was reading his chest. He quickly turned over and pulled his pillow over his head.

There was a long silence that was broken by Billy's father. "William, please turn over and tell me what the heck, I WAS MURDERED—TGD 3UE—LOOK IN TRUNK—HIJACKERS means and why it's written on your chest in felt pen."

Billy felt the blood drain from his face as if it were trying to escape what was coming. He scrambled for a lie to make the words on his chest reasonable and logical. There was nothing. There was less than nothing. It was like the last strand holding him together had suddenly snapped and his whole being was flooding out. Billy sat up and the tears flowed down his face. He had no words. In place of words were sobs carrying great gouts of sound without meaning.

"William, what happened? Tell me. I can help. I can make it all better. I know I can. Tell me. Are you alright?" he pled and looked more carefully at Billy. He saw his foot wrapped up in toilet paper and took it off. He inspected his foot. "This cut is very bad. You will need stitches. He grabbed Billy, held him until he stopped sobbing and kept repeating that everything would be alright.

The fear slowly ebbed, and Billy pushed away from his father. "I'm okay, Dad," he said.

"Good," replied his father. "Now get up and get dressed. Have breakfast and tell me what happened."

Billy sat at the breakfast table, and his dad sat a pile of steaming hot blueberry pancakes down in front of him. Billy looked up. "I didn't know you could make pancakes," he said and smiled.

"It is a well-guarded secret," said his dad with a grin. "Now eat and tell me what happened last night."

Billy started with the secret passage over the maple tree to the fort up the cedar tree on the Cooper property. He told him about finding the buckle with the skeleton and finding the tunnel and the cupboard in the cellar that opened on a bricked-up passageway. He told his dad how the buckle with the Chinese lettering had led him to the trapdoor in the shed and how he had opened it. He explained the lights he had connected in the tunnel and the gate and the lock and crossing the freeway at night to look for the key to the lock. He explained all of what he had done without telling his dad about the hijackers.

"William, that does not explain what happened," said his dad.

"I know," said Billy, feeling a great relief a sharing his

adventures. "There is more. Jackie and I spent the first night in the tree fort. We saw some cops pull over a semi on the freeway. The cops acted strange. We realized that they were not real cops. They had an unmarked car, and they pulled over a big rig carrying valuable cargo and hijacked it. We were afraid adults would not believe us and would take away our secret tree house, so we didn't say anything. We tried to get evidence to show you after the summer was over by setting up a motion activated camera to record another hijacking. Jackie borrowed a camera from his dad, but his dad found out it was missing and made him return it. He got grounded because of it."

"Please get to how and why you cut your foot and wrote that on your chest."

"Well, I had kind of forgotten about the hijackers. I didn't tell Jackie about the secret tunnel. I wanted to keep it for myself. After going to the university and hearing about the gang of Chinese men and how they might have used the forge to melt down their stolen gold, I thought there might still be gold down in the tunnel, so I decided to find it myself." His father nodded. There was a slight hint of a smile at the corner of his mouth, but it was soon replaced by a stern frown.

"I couldn't find any key to the gate, so I figured it had

to be on the other side. I told you I was going to camp out with the gang, but I went by myself and hid in the shed. I turned on my light string and went over the freeway to find the other end of the tunnel and maybe find the key and the gold. I was looking for the opening on the median when I heard a semi stop and saw flashing police lights. I went to look, but as I was peeking out of the bushes I slipped and fell. That is when the hijackers caught me and threw me in the trunk of their car." Billy stared at the look of horror on his father's face. He continued. "I heard them plan to kill me by hitting me on the head and drowning me in a lake, so I wrote a message in the trunk and wrote this note on my chest, so whoever found me would know I had been murdered."

His dad was wide-eyed, shocked at the thought.

Billy filled in all the details of his time in the trunk of the car, his escape, and his finding the key to the lock in the cave. Billy felt so good to finally be telling someone. He even smiled as he explained cutting the tape from his hands, running away, and cutting his foot. Billy's dad did not scold or chastise him for his bad choices, but Billy knew that would come later. He was going to have to pay for not telling his father. It would not be pleasant, but it would be fair. Billy would accept whatever punishment his father decided.

HIJACKED

As far as the hijackers were concerned, Billy would spend three hours explaining to the police everything he had seen. The license plate number he had written on his chest was the most important piece of evidence. The real police found the fake cop car. In the trunk was the note Billy had written. That enabled the police to get search warrants for a number of properties, and the hijackers were arrested. There was never any mention of Billy's name during the trial. His name and phone number were redacted from the evidence given at the trial. He would be safe from any of the hijackers ever finding out his identity.

There was only one thing he held back. He simply left it out, rationalizing that it was okay to omit a small detail from the story—one that wouldn't hurt anyone. So, he kept it to himself. The omission was easy to maintain: concealed under a loose floorboard in his bedroom was a small box with 12 gold bars painted black with a Chinese house marking imprinted into each one. Billy looked it up on his dad's computer.

The symbol was the Chinese word for gold. He erased his browsing history from his dad's computer.

acknowledgements

I would like to thank my wife, Cheryl, for her honesty, without which I would have surely gotten lost in the words; my daughters who showed me the importance of being a good father; and my editor at Night Owl Freelance, Vanessa Anderson, for patching the holes.

Be on the lookout for the next
beechwood adventure
at IndieOwlPress.com!

ABOUT THE AUTHOR

G. MICHAEL SMITH is a retired teacher of Computer Programming, Drama, Math, English, and Theatre. He's written and directed plays for both adults and children. He also writes poetry and novels.

His body of work includes *The Forever Series*, consisting of *Fixer 13, Master Fixer, Impostor, Omie 17*, and the forthcoming fifth book in the series, *WU*. He is also currently working on *The Power and the Glory: A Man-made Tale*.

His children's book publications include *Lily Liar*, and *The Accidental Adventures of Bernie the Banana Slug*, and forthcoming *Tiny Tina*, as well as *Ashley and the Hornets*.

He resides in Qualicum Beach, Vancouver Island, BC, Canada with his wife, Cheryl, and enjoys spending time with his three adult daughters and three grandchildren. He's also known to enjoy a rigorous game of pickleball, softball, squash, or badminton.